LOVE
to GO

TAKE A CHANCE, BOOK 5

Nancy Warren

AMBLESIDE PUBLISHING

Love to Go
Take a Chance: Book Five
Copyright © 2016 Nancy Weatherley Warren
All rights reserved

Discover other titles by Nancy Warren at
www.NancyWarren.net

ONE

MARGUERITE CHANCE STEPPED out onto the front porch of her small cottage, her purple yoga mat under one arm and her first cup of green tea in her hand. Luckily, the porch was a covered one, for rain was coming down in a misty curtain, so her flower garden looked like a soggy impressionist painting. The trellis tumbled with heirloom roses, their pink and white blooms drooping wetly. Beyond the garden was the bulk of her world. Fields of organic vegetables stretched out in rows, lush and heavy with bounty.

It was late September in Hidden Falls, Oregon; harvest time. This rain marked the end of a long stretch of sunshine during which she and her casual farm laborers had picked fresh lettuce, tomatoes, some of the squash, beans and kale. Her shoulders and back ached from the exertion, but it was a good ache. The greens had likely already been eaten in the high-end restaurants that bought most of her organic heirloom produce.

She rolled out her mat on the porch, ready for her

morning yoga session, and then settled into the old rocker that sat near the door to drink her tea and simply to enjoy this quiet moment so early in the day. As soon as she sat, Ophelia, a young black and white cat that she'd found half drowned and brought home, strolled past rubbing against her knees and then slowly, and oh-so-casually, turned and jumped into her lap.

She rocked slowly in the wicker chair on the porch, Ophelia a warm, purring comfort. Rain dripped from the eaves and the moist morning air was heavy with the smells of damp earth and late summer flowers. Her rocker creaked slightly against the wooden porch. Her dad had built the porch himself, which was why none of the boards fit quite evenly. From her small cottage she could just see the house where she'd grown up. As she watched, a beat-up Jeep rattled up the gravel road toward her. It slowed and came to a stop and her dad rolled down the window, letting out a blast of Jumping Jack Flash. "How's my beautiful girl?" he bellowed, cheerful in spite of the weather.

Since she was the only one of their eleven kids living on the property, Jack Chance always seemed happy to see her. "I'm fine. Do want some tea?"

"Can't. I'm helping build a barn." Jack loved to build things. But his skills were never as grand as his visions. She only hoped there were more experienced barn builders going today to keep him in check.

"Have fun."

"You know, seeing you there reminds me of

Daphne's great aunt Mildred. She used to sit right there on that porch in that very rocker when she got old and the kids were too much for her." He shook his head. "Sure takes me back." Then he waved, rolled the window back up and drove on.

She stared after the departing Jeep that was streaked with dust and rain. She reminded him of great aunt Mildred? She was twenty-eight years old. Was she really beginning to act like an ancient spinster? She pictured herself sitting here in a rocker with the cat in her lap. Her tea. Her garden. Could she be any more of a cliché?

She'd put down roots here from the moment she was born.

She'd always loved this land from when she was a tiny girl and she'd helped her mom and dad tend the gardens and the chickens. When the rental cottage on the property became available two years ago, it had seemed natural that she should take it over. It wasn't as though she had never left home. She'd opted, instead of college, to travel around Europe and Australia working on organic farms, sometimes volunteering her time for free and sometimes being paid a pittance. She'd learned a lot about farming and had an opportunity to see the world. While working on a farm in rural France she'd learned French. As much as she'd loved her time away, she'd been very happy to return home. She wasn't one who craved excitement and new things. She liked to be around familiar places and people she knew. She loved watching the seasons change and the crops she planted grow and flourish. She liked living in a community where most everyone knew everyone else. At one time she had worried that she had so few ambitions but she had figured out a way to make a life for herself with a small business that would never make her rich but allowed her to live a life that was meaningful to her.

"You're as rooted here as those lumpy tomatoes you grow," her younger, restless brother Cooper had told her one day. To him her life was no doubt boring, but to her it was exactly what she wanted. Maybe she was lonely, once in a while, but the feeling usually passed.

She stood, replacing the protesting cat on the seat cushion, and proceeded to do a series of sun salutations. Rain salutations, really, but the land needed rain as well as sun and there was a kind of wet beauty in the dripping landscape. Stretched and invigorated, she swapped yoga pants for an old pair of jeans, left her long hair tied back—much easier than dealing with the mess of curls—and headed to the shed where crates of produce were waiting. Her main clients had all received their deliveries yesterday, but she had a few personal deliveries to make herself this morning. She hefted stacks of wooden crates into the bed of her faded and dusty red truck and was on her way.

Her first stop was the Sunflower Coffee and Tea Company, the bakery and café where her sister Iris baked and served the best muffins and goodies in town. She timed her visit strategically to coincide with the end of the morning rush. She was an early riser but she had nothing on Iris, who was baking by five and open by six. It was after nine, now. The workers dashing in for a coffee on their way to the office, followed by the heading-to-school crowd, was over. Tinkling chimes above the door announced her arrival as she backed into the cafe, her arms laden with the box of fragrant purple blueberries. She glanced around. A group of exhausted-looking young mothers with toddlers sat around a big table mainlining coffee. A couple of older men faced each other in a corner arguing about something in gruff voices, politics it sounded like, but otherwise Sunflower was empty. She approached the counter where Iris was replenishing her signature brownies in the glass display case. She glanced up and smiled when she saw her sister. "Hey, sis. Is that box full of what I think it is?"

"It is." The smell of fresh blueberries emanated from the box like a fruity aphrodisiac.

Iris nodded, peeking into the box with a professional eye. "I've got a few recipes in mind for these. I thought I might try baking those open blueberry tarts like they do in France."

"I only grow the berries. I don't consult on cooking methods." Marguerite glanced around. "Where do you want them?"

"Bring them through to the kitchen."

She carried the box behind the counter and into the kitchen, a scene of organized chaos that told how busy Iris's mornings were. Pans and trays were stacked at the industrial sink waiting to be washed, flour dusted not only the work surfaces but also the floor, and tantalizing smells emanated from the ovens. "I don't know how you do it," she said, amazed as always at how Iris managed to run such a hectic business.

"I go without sleep." As though on cue, she yawned, hugely. "Do you have time to stop? Morning Glory muffins are just out of the oven."

"I skipped breakfast for a reason. And I always have time for you."

Iris nodded. "It's one of the nicest things about you, you're probably the only person I know who always has time. You're never in a hurry, are you?"

Coming from Iris, who was run off her feet, the comment made her feel lazy. She shrugged. "I don't like feeling rushed. When you grow produce for living, you get used to a slower pace."

"My life is exactly opposite. When you sling coffee and muffins to rushing commuters and the early bird crowd, you get used to a very fast pace." Hidden Falls was a small town, but enough of its population commuted to larger work centers, and wanted a good coffee to take with them, that Iris sometimes had lines as long as a Seattle Starbucks.

Iris fixed them both an herbal tea, which she carried to a vacant table. Marguerite followed with the muffins. They settled across from each other. Even though they saw each other most days, they never ran out of things to talk about. They were close in age, similar in temperament and had remained best friends all their lives.

That's why she knew that her sister had something important to say. You didn't know a woman all her life, call her sister, and not recognize the signs. Iris's cheeks were glowing, which suggested the news was good. She shifted the pottery bowl containing packets of sugar and sweetener, and fiddled with the edges of her muffin. The diamond on her engagement ring winked as her restless hands stayed busy. Marguerite simply waited, knowing that Iris would tell her what was on her mind when she was ready. Finally, her sister leaned forward and said, "I have to tell someone. I wanted you to be the first."

She nodded, feeling a growing sense of anticipation since she was pretty sure she had an idea about the good news that was to come.

Iris glanced around to make sure they weren't overheard, then dropped her voice. "Marguerite, we did it!"

She leaned in, mirroring her sister's posture and whispered back, "That's fantastic. Did you do what I think you did?" She wanted to be absolutely certain before giving out congratulations.

Iris nodded, her eyes filling with sudden tears. "We're going to have a baby! Me and Geoff, we're going to have a child."

She felt her own eyes fill. She knew how much this meant to Iris, who, less than a year ago, had decided to have a child on her own. And now here she was with the man of her dreams about to have that baby she wanted so much. "I am so happy for you."

"Thanks. I can't believe it's real."

"How does Geoff feel?"

"I think he's as excited as I am."

When Geoff McLeod had moved to Hidden Falls as the new high school English teacher, he and Iris had hit it off right away, and Marguerite along with most everyone in town had seen that they were perfect for each other. Iris was a published author as well as a bakery owner, but their path hadn't been a smooth one. However, once they committed to each other, they were a solid, happy couple. And now they were having a child together.

"How do you feel?"

"Exhausted. I could curl up under this table and sleep for ten hours." She grinned. "Which is a great sign. I've never been so happy to be tired. Now, if I could only start being sick in the morning my life would be perfect."

Marguerite was still bubbling with excitement when she drove into Portland. She didn't do many deliveries herself, but she made sure to take a route at least once a month so she could visit the restaurants that stocked her produce and chat with the chefs. Sometimes they wanted her to try her hand at some fruit or veg she'd never heard of but more often they wanted more of something. As she began to plan her plantings for the next year, it was good to hear from her customers what they wanted.

No one knew better than a top chef the importance

of good produce. She timed her last stop so she got to the bank of food trucks after the lunch rush was over and the dinner rush hadn't yet begun. She pulled into the parking area in the middle and hauled out two boxes of beautiful fresh heirloom tomatoes. She hefted them to Alexei's Greek food truck. Alexei Vasilopoulos cooked some of the best Greek food this side of Athens. He was also the brother of her sister Rose's boyfriend and, unfortunately for Marguerite, the most beautiful man on earth.

Her pulse kicked up a notch as she approached the food truck. Melissa, Alexei's assistant, wasn't around but she could see the back of Alexei. Before he turned and saw her she took a moment simply to drink in the sight of him. Even from the back he was the best-looking man she had ever gazed upon. He was tall, with broad shoulders that tapered to a lean waist and hips. She could see the muscles of his back shifting as he worked. She didn't get nearly long enough to admire his beauty before, as though he felt her presence, he turned and the impact of his utter gorgeousness struck her as it always did.

Each time, after she'd seen him, she'd go away and think she'd exaggerated his perfection in her head; no man could really be that beautiful. And then she'd see him and realize that her memory was only playing tricks in that it didn't do him justice. Glossy, curly hair, almond shaped eyes that were a curious shade between brown and green that tilted at the corners as though he was always thinking sensuous thoughts, a straight and classical nose, firm jaw and lips that could have been chiseled by a sculptor. And then there was his body.

He was so utterly perfect that it wasn't fair. No one ever made her feel quite so ordinary as he did. Marguerite had never been a beauty and it had never bothered her before. But when he turned his Greek god's gaze upon her she felt like a mere mortal and a very ordinary woman.

When he looked at her, she was dazzled by the impact of those gorgeous eyes. There was just the one dimple when he smiled but instead of seeming like an imperfection—one dimple, not two—that tiny flaw only added to his appeal.

He looked at her as though she was beautiful and desirable but that could only be her own feelings reflecting back at her. "Hey, Marguerite," he said. "Did you bring me something special?"

"I like to think so." And she placed the box on the counter. Instead of taking the box with a quick thanks and pushing them into the corner as she had expected, he motioned her to climb into the side door of the truck. When she did, feeling her pulse kick up a notch just being in the small space with him, he reached into the box and took out one of the tomatoes, inspecting it as though it were an engagement ring he was thinking about purchasing.

He rubbed his hand over the glossy red surface, brought the brilliant red fruit to his nose and inhaled deeply. Watching him was one of the most sensuous things she had ever experienced. He closed his eyes and she knew that he loved food and freshly grown produce with the same passion she did. He said, "You can almost smell the earth and the water, and the winds and the rains of Oregon."

Her smile bloomed. "I know! I feel the same way." She rummaged in the box and pulled out some of the lumpy heirloom varieties that she felt had the most flavor. "You have to try this purple one. It's an old varietal. I wasn't sure how well it would do in this climate but I think the results are spectacular."

"After the morning I've had, it's great to get some good news."

She nodded. "It was stressful. I can see it in your shoulders. You're holding them around your ears." She put down the tomato and placed her hands on his shoulders, pressing down lightly. He watched her from those amazing eyes and, even as she talked about relaxation, tension built low in her belly. Still, she kept her breathing deep and slow and felt him follow suit. Beneath her palms his shoulders dropped. She rubbed them lightly, feeling the tense muscles begin to ease.

"If all suppliers were like you, I'd be a Zen master."

She chuckled, "No, you wouldn't. You'd never be able to sit still long enough."

"True."

She stepped away, still feeling the warmth from his shoulders in her palms.

"I had to fire a guy this morning. He's been stealing from me. Which sucks, especially as hiring him was a favor to a friend. He's fighting a drug problem. Promised he was clean and sober, but ..."

"I'm sorry."

"I'm trying to expand, but without good staff, I'm stuck."

"And you hate to be stuck." They hadn't known each other long, they'd met through his brother and her sister only a few months ago but she felt as though she'd known him forever. When they'd first started emailing the topic had been food. They talked about the slow food movement, the local food movement, the food truck movement. He had big plans to expand his empire. She got the feeling that he hated to be still. Even his work was on wheels!

"Yeah."

He retrieved the deep purple tomato and drew out one of his sharp knives. With clean efficiency he sliced the tomato into slices, passed her one and bit into another himself with strong white teeth.

She bit into her slice and, even though she'd been eating them for days, still experienced the spurt of flavor and the intensity of taste which, if possible, tasted even more exquisite since she was sharing it with someone else who appreciated fresh, simple food the way she did.

He nodded, looking blissed out. Then he said, "I can't believe how good that tastes. I wish you had boxes and boxes."

"I do, too. Next year we'll plant more. But I wanted you to try these."

"Thanks." His eyes glowed when he looked at her. "I have something for you, too."

"You do?"

He reached onto an upper shelf and brought down a glass bottle. It didn't look like the kind of bottle you purchased from the local grocer. When she raised her brows he said, "It's olive oil. My uncle grows the olives and makes oil in small batches. He also ships me the olives that I use."

He handed her the bottle and then said, "Wait, let me show you." He reached into the box of tomatoes, dug around for another heirloom variety, sliced it and then opened the bottle and drizzled oil over the slices. He passed her one and when she bit into the tomato she felt the flavors meld and nearly moaned. She felt Alexei watching her and when their gazes connected she felt something hot flash between them. No, no, no. Hot made her think of fire. Which reminded her of getting burned!

TWO

"HONESTLY, IT WAS so intimate it felt like we were having sex or something," she told Iris. She'd driven straight to her sister's since she had to tell someone. "Well, it's been so long since I had sex that I'm probably wrong, but it was definitely a moment of intimacy."

"Then what did you do?" Iris was alight with curiosity. Well, she was alight with a lot of things. New life and possibilities and the happiness of knowing she was going to be a mom. Something she'd always wanted.

"A customer arrived. A pretty redhead who looked at Alexei like he was on the menu." She tried to accept that it was a good thing they'd been interrupted. "He's a gorgeous man who can't help the way he looks. Women drool over him all the time. Part of his gift is that he looks at every female as though she's the only one on earth. It's incredible. And I'm so ordinary. Being around him reminds me of all those Greek myths where the mortal woman who messes with the gorgeous Greek god ends up being turned into a bush or something. So I left."

Iris had been following every word with an eager expression while she expertly arranged freshly baked chocolate cookies with white chocolate chunks in the display case, and now she dropped one so it fell on its side and broke in two. Iris was never clumsy. From her stunned expression it was clear that she could not believe the words she was hearing. "You got out of there? And here I was picturing him leaning across oh, so slowly, and wiping his thumb across your bottom lip, where it was slick with olive oil, and then licking his thumb."

"Would you stop it?" Marguerite could feel her face heating, mostly because that was pretty much the same fantasy she'd been indulging. Naturally, in her fantasy, he took the oil and.... No. She had to stop it.

Her sister picked up the two pieces of broken cookie and handed them to Marguerite. "Here, you might as well eat this since you made me break it."

"Thanks." She felt like she needed all the chocolate she could gobble right now.

While she munched, Iris finished putting out the cookies and then a couple of teenagers came in and ordered the day's coffee special, so she expertly whipped up two salted caramel lattes. When they'd gone, Iris turned back to her. "I think you're making him out to be way more hot than he really is. You're a good looking woman, don't sell yourself short."

"No. Really. It's impossible to describe how

gorgeous he is until you've seen him."

The ringing of the bells signaled a new arrival into the cafe, and there was their mom striding in with a big smile on her face.

"Not a word," Iris whispered. She nodded fast, but Daphne hadn't brought up eleven kids without learning to read lips, or use some psychic mom power only she could access. "Not a word about what?" she asked.

Iris had always been faster on her feet than Marguerite. She said, "Marguerite's got a crush on a food truck guy, but she doesn't want anyone to know."

As a way of deflecting their mom, this was a pretty good ploy, but Marguerite really didn't appreciate being thrown under the bus—or the food truck. "Iris!" she hissed in her most menacing tone, which was about as menacing as a tiny kitten's meow.

"Do you mean Alexei? Well, that's not news," Daphne said cheerfully. "Every woman has a crush on him. That boy is sex on legs."

"See?" Marguerite said, looking significantly at her sister, "I told you."

"Come on," Iris said, "He can't be that gorgeous."

Daphne fanned her face with her hand. "Oh, honey, he is. I have never seen a more beautiful man. He's like a movie star except he doesn't need airbrushing." She sighed deeply. "And he can cook. You and Geoff should go there. Take a day off for a change and drive into Portland. You could visit Rose and then go to Alexei's. He makes the best Greek food."

"And I don't have a crush on him." Marguerite felt it was important to make this point clear.

Her mom turned to stare at her. "Then you need your hormone levels checked." Daphne's blue-green eyes began to dance. "Besides, he definitely has a crush on you."

"No. He doesn't. He's the most gorgeous man on the planet and I'm a frumpy woman with dirt under her fingernails."

"Also cat hair all over your sweater," her sister added. "Just being helpful in case, you know, you're going to see him again."

She brushed at her sweater but there wasn't much point. He'd already seen her like this.

"You're an Earth-mother type, darling," Daphne reminded her. "It's who you are and a lot of men find that very attractive."

"Not the most gorgeous man on the planet." She bit into the other half of the broken cookie.

Daphne suddenly leaned across the bakery counter and touched the back of her hand to Iris's face. "Are you feeling all right, honey?"

Iris glanced at Marguerite in near panic before returning her gaze to her mother's concerned countenance. It really was spooky how their mom could see right into them. "I'm feel fine, Mom. Maybe a little sleep-deprived."

Daphne did not look convinced but before she could pry, which was pretty much her favorite activity, the bell rang again to announce the arrival of Geoff, carrying a beat-up brown leather briefcase and wearing a tweed jacket over jeans. He was handsome in a low-key way with light brown hair, big blue eyes and an easy way about him. Even though he and Iris had been together for less than a year, he'd become solidly part of the family and was one of Marguerite's favorite people. He usually dropped by Sunflower on his way home from school unless he was working late, so no one was surprised to see him.

His eyes went straight to Iris, and when she saw the intimate way they looked at each other she quickly glanced away as though she was witnessing something she wasn't meant to see. Daphne was not so tactful. She openly grinned watching her daughter and the man she loved. She added to her tact by commenting aloud, "Isn't it wonderful to see two people so much in love?" She put her hand to her chest. "You two remind me of Jack and me when we were young and in love."

"If you mean acting all lovey and inappropriate in front of other people, you still do that."

Daphne chuckled. "I guess we do. Jack's such an open-hearted man and he loves to show his affection. I've got used to it."

"Did you show up for any reason other than to embarrass us, Mom?" Iris asked.

"Yes, yes I did. Thanks for reminding me. I want to order some baked goods for the Fall Harvest Fair meeting on Thursday." Her gold curls, threaded lightly with gray, bounced as she looked from one to the other of her daughters. "Embarrassing you both is just one of the joys of being a mother."

Geoff chuckled but Iris and Marguerite rolled their eyes in unison.

"I'd like three dozen muffins and a dozen lemon bars and a dozen cookies. Assorted, whatever you have."

Iris grabbed a notepad and scribbled the order. "What time for pickup?"

"Ten in the morning?"

"Sure. I'll have the stuff ready. Ten on Thursday."

"Fantastic."

"Do you want some tea or something, Mom?"

She checked her watch, a silver piece with an enormous face. "Can't. I've got to pick up an order of clay. I'm nearly out. Well, I'll let you two girls get back to whatever you were really talking about when I came in." With a wave she headed back out the way she came. Once she was gone Iris let out a breath. "That freaks me out. I swear she knows everything."

Marguerite nodded. "She always did. Why don't you just tell her?"

Geoff said, "I agree. And why don't you sit down?" He motioned with his hand. "I can put on an apron and man the counter while you two settle down and talk this out." The glance he sent Marguerite suggested that she was supposed to talk Iris into putting her feet up for the next nine months, which she knew, as well as Geoff probably did, was never going to happen.

"Now that Mom's gone, can I just say, congratulations," she said to Geoff, opening her arms wide.

His infectious grin was so bright it almost cast a shadow. "You sure can," he replied and enveloped her in a bear hug.

"I am so happy for both of you."

Iris nodded. "Thanks. I'll get our drinks."

Geoff walked around the back of the bakery case and physically pushed Iris out from behind it towards where Marguerite was watching in amusement. "I'll get it. What do you want, Marguerite?"

She was tempted to walk behind the counter and get their tea herself since she was perfectly capable of operating the fancy barista machine, but she understood that he needed to prove to Iris that he was the kind of man who could make tea. Hopefully, he was also the kind of man who could change a diaper, feed a kid a bottle and whatever mysterious other things new parents had to do, all of which they were going to have to figure out pretty soon. She said, "Whatever kind of green tea there is would be perfect, thank you."

"Now go and sit down," he ordered.

When the two women had settled at their favorite table in the back by the window, Iris said, "That man is going to turn into a control freak, isn't he?"

"I think he wants you to be healthy," Marguerite said. "He might be a bit overprotective at first while he gets used to the idea."

"I guess."

Then she repeated her question from earlier. "Why

aren't you telling Mom? Do you have any idea how thrilled she'll be? She knows how much you've always wanted a baby."

Iris ran a hand over her face. "It's so hard to explain. I know how happy she'll be but this news is so new and Geoff and I have barely had time to take it in ourselves. I'm not ready to tell everybody. I mean, what if something went wrong? Things can go wrong, right?"

She heard the note of anxiety in her sister's tone and had no idea how to respond. She took a moment before saying, "Of course they can. But, you're a healthy woman. Why do you think something would go wrong?"

"Because I want this baby so badly. Because if I tell Mom and the rest of the family then it's not a happy secret any more, it's planning baby showers and picking out names and everybody secretly wondering if Geoff and I will get married and—and suddenly it's real and then if it doesn't work out it will be so much bigger a disaster."

Marguerite reached over and took her sister's hand. Sometimes, she knew, there was no easy answer, no promise she could give that everything would be all right. All she could do was give her silent support. No, not silent. She said, "I will always be there for you. I know there are no guarantees in life but I think it's going to be okay. I do."

Iris squeezed her hand. "God, I hope so. I've never wanted anything as much as I want this. Well, maybe I wanted Geoff this badly."

"So, I guess it would be a little early to talk about names? And you know I'm already planning the baby shower in my head."

At least she got a laugh. "You see? You're bad enough. Can you even imagine what Mom's going to be like?"

"When are you planning to tell them?"

"I have my first scan in a couple of weeks. I think, if everything looks good then we'll tell them. Maybe at one of Mom's Sunday dinners. We'll get the news out of the way at once and tell everybody."

Geoff brought their tea up at that moment. Iris reached out to take his hand with a quick word of thanks. Marguerite loved to see these two. If there was ever a couple who made you believe in forever love it had to be Iris and Geoff. So far, she hadn't asked the obvious question. Were they going to get married?

As Geoff set the cups down, Iris said, "Sit down and join us, why don't you? We're done with the secretive girl talk now."

He glanced at Marguerite, "Are you sure you don't mind?"

She grinned at him. "You're going to be the father of my new niece or nephew. I'd be happy to have tea with you."

His whole face lit up at the word *father*. "I still can't believe it. A year ago I came to this town broken and sorry for myself and starting over and now I've found an amazing woman and I'm going to be a dad. I even like the kids I teach in my high school. How great is that?"

She chuckled. "It's probably a good quality in a teacher. I think it's good that you like your kids. And you like your job. And you like this town. But mostly, I'm happy that you love my sister."

He took Iris's hand. "That I do."

Iris said, "I'll be glad when the scan is done. I feel like everything is going so fast. Like some alien's taken over my body. I'm only about six weeks along but I swear my stomach is already starting to bulge."

Geoff watched as Iris's hand settled on her belly. "Are you sure you should be doing all this extra baking? I really think you need to rest more. Marguerite, don't you agree with me?" His face creased with concern. "Iris should be sitting down more. She works too hard. All this stress and long hours can't be good for the baby."

Her sister let out a breath as though this was an argument they'd had more than once. She said, "Geoff, being pregnant is a normal part of life. My doctor says I'm fine to continue working so long as I feel good."

"I think you should tell your mother about the baby. You should tell your family, so they can help you. And we need more staff."

Iris nodded. "I know we need more staff. I am keeping my eyes open." She glanced at Marguerite. "I figure when I get towards the end and I'm as big as a house I'm going to want to take it more easy. Plus, of course, I'll want to take time off when the baby comes.

But it's so hard to find anybody in the area who can bake and is good with customers."

"What about Dosana?" Marguerite asked. Dosana was a young business graduate who had become Iris's right hand.

Iris shook her head. "She's got her hands full with the second bakery. Maybe we shouldn't have expanded so soon, but I didn't know I was going to get pregnant." And she glanced to Geoff with an impish grin that lit up her face, "Though I'm sure glad I did."

Geoff rubbed her shoulders with a protective hand. "Me too. I've never been happier about anything in my life."

Marguerite said, "You know I'll help out where I can. But I've got to get all the harvest in. Plus, my area of expertise is growing vegetables. I can't bake anything. I burn toast."

Iris nodded. "I know. You would have been my first choice except for the fact that you have absolutely zero talent as a baker. No, I'm going to have to start widening my search. Put the word out for someone who can help. Even extra orders like the one from Mom mean I get a little less sleep. I can't believe the Fall Harvest Festival is already here. I don't know where this year has gone."

Marguerite nodded. "I know. It feels like every year goes faster. Plus, you had a pretty busy time, opening a second bakery and well, making babies and all."

Iris grinned. "The making babies was definitely

the best part."

Marguerite put her hands over her head in exaggerated shock. "Don't remind me. I feel like everybody in my family is having excellent sex except for me."

"Well, not everyone."

"There's you, disgustingly happy growing babies, there's Prescott and Holly, Evan and Caitlyn. Even Rose, pickiest woman on the planet, seems to have found her dream guy." And that dream guy had an even dreamier brother. Seemed like it was a combination of seeing her brothers and sisters finding love and happiness and always feeling like she was hidden away that was giving her this strange sense of loss. "Even my Mom is getting more than I am. Plus, when Dad drove by my cottage this morning and I was sitting outside on the rocker, he said I reminded him of Great Aunt Mildred. And I think he meant it like that was a good thing!"

Iris laughed, long and hard, so she had to bend over in her chair. "Oh, Dad has to be the most clueless man sometimes. You know he didn't mean that in a bad way."

"How is it good that I'm twenty-eight and remind him of an eighty-something year old spinster?"

Instead of answering, Iris said, "Maybe you need to get out more. I mean, you're tucked away in a little cottage like Snow White." Her eyes began to dance. "You even have seven dwarves—well at least seven dwarves, all those random gardening guys who come and pick the produce. They're definitely a motley crew."

She winced. "I know, but Snow White? Really?"

Iris shrugged. "Snow White got her prince."

"Yes. But she nearly died of food poisoning first."

"True. Well, here's my advice, move out of the cottage into town. Or, I don't know, start spending some weekends in Portland or Seattle. Find someplace where there are men. Have you tried Internet dating?"

"No. I have not tried online dating. And I don't want to. I believe that there's somebody out there for everybody."

"I do, too, but how are they supposed to find you? Maybe you should put out a road sign. *Stop here for fresh organic produce and a hot, single gardener.*"

Marguerite snorted with laughter. "Oh stop it. And don't mention the idea to Mom because you know she'd do it."

Geoff chimed in, "Daphne would walk up and down wearing a sandwich board if it would make you happy."

"I know. She's a great mom but she does get enthusiastic about her projects. Luckily with so many kids it's easy to get her focus transferred to somebody else." Marguerite eyed Iris's still flat stomach and said, "Like this new baby."

Iris raised a finger. "You are not allowed to tell Daphne. Do you understand?"

"Of course I do. But she'll find out eventually." Then an awful thought struck her. "Do you think she'll take up knitting?"

Iris groaned and put her head in her hand. "If her knitting is like her pottery, my poor kid will look like a sock puppet."

"We have to head her off. No knitting. I know, why don't you suggest that she make a pottery statue to celebrate the birth of your child. Maybe a fountain? Something complicated that would take her months."

Since Daphne was an enthusiastic potter this seemed like an excellent idea. "Thanks, I'll keep that in mind. And you should think about what I said about getting out more."

"I know."

"You're sure the food truck guy—"

"No! Mom thinks every man has a crush on us, you know that. He is a friend, but he is definitely not interested in me."

"Then he's a fool," Geoff said. Which was one of the reasons she loved him. He was definitely the brother she'd never had. Not that she didn't have plenty of brothers, and she loved every one of them, but they weren't given to pumping up a girl's ego.

THREE

AS MARGUERITE HEADED home, a paper bag containing two morning glory muffins under her arm, she noticed the changing leaves. She loved fall for its bounty and the rich, colorful produce, but the season also reminded her that winter was on its way. Autumn was when her busy season ended and she had time. Time to peruse seed catalogs and get to the projects she'd been putting off for months. Not that she really had a lot of projects this year. She had kind of a restless feeling deep in her belly.

It wasn't that she was jealous of Iris; on the contrary, she was so happy she couldn't keep the grin off her face. Iris had always wanted children and for a while it seemed like motherhood might not be in the cards. She could still remember sitting with her sister considering likely candidates for artificial insemination. And then Geoff had moved to Hidden Falls and changed everything.

Maybe that was where the restless feeling was coming from, knowing that another year had passed her by. Marguerite was earthy in every possible way. She was also a sensuous woman, but unfortunately she had the worst taste in men.

During her year studying organic farming, she'd had many amazing experiences, but there were some bitter memories associated with her time abroad also. Mostly because of a guy named Timothy. Tim had been another budding organic farmer. She'd met him in Australia. At the time, he was the best-looking man she had ever seen or believed existed. A tall, lanky Aussie, she still remembered his bright blue eyes, and how they twinkled when they looked at her as though they shared some private joke. His blond, sun-bleached hair was permanently tousled as though he'd just rolled out of bed, and he'd sported sexy stubble all day long.

Only once she'd known him had she realized that he worked at his casual look. He had the body of a surfer, tanned and fit, and a joking manner that had quite literally melted the panties off her. Their affair had been intense and magical. Tim had made her believe in love as she'd never believed in it before. He'd promised to come home with her, and they'd made plans far into the night. They'd build their own farm together, he'd talked about marriage so that she could stay in Australia or he could come to North America. For three glorious, perfect months she had been deliriously happy, believing she had found the man of her dreams. And then, like all dreams, this one ended. And with a wake-up that had been painful and brutal.

It turned out she wasn't the only woman he was seeing, the only woman he was making promises to. With a broken heart, she'd cried into a few beers too many in a local pub and one of the other girls she'd been working with said words that had stuck with her forever. "A man that good-looking, you're never going to keep him on a leash. He's like a gift, Darl. No woman can resist a man like that. You can't really blame him. If you want a man who sticks, aim lower."

So she'd hauled her broken heart back home with her along with a few very good skills she had acquired and she had retreated into her cottage and put her heart and soul into nurturing plants, creating new life in the form of heirloom tomatoes and sunburst squashes.

That was two years ago and she hadn't had a serious relationship since.

She arrived home in a pensive mood. Ophelia was curled in the rocking chair on the porch and leapt down to wind around her feet meowing plaintively. She scooped the cat up, and while the little black and white body purred loudly in her ear, its body hanging over her shoulder, she entered her small cottage.

There were times when she would flip through Architectural Digest in a doctor's waiting room or see a chic New York apartment in a magazine layout or on television and she would long for a moment for that sophisticated lifestyle. The sleek edges and a high-powered job and the wardrobe and everything that went with it. But, when she looked around her cottage and saw the decor that was more shabby than chic, the solid wood pieces she'd refinished herself, the comfy chintz couches and chairs, she felt at home in a way that a New York loft never would.

"Do I seem dull?" she asked the cat. Ophelia made a small sound like a burble which she took to be a yes. She filled a small bowl with food and freshened a dish of water and left her companion crunching happily. Marguerite walked to her computer. First she checked the restaurant orders for the upcoming week. But one email in her inbox jumped out at her: from Alexei's Greek.

A sizzle of excitement coursed through her body just seeing his email address. The header was Juicy Tomatoes. In another man and in another context she felt *juicy tomatoes* could be a bit of a sexy come on. With Alexei she knew he was referring to organic produce. Still, she eagerly clicked on the message. It said:

Dear Marguerite, I don't think I have ever tasted tomatoes quite so fresh and rich flavored as the heirloom varieties you brought over today.

She was completely overwhelmed. For him to rave about tomatoes was praise that mattered to her. He was, like all good chefs, demanding and incredibly picky.

Of course, there weren't enough to use in my regular Greek salads, so I devised a little something that I hope you'll approve of. I called it Tomatoes Marguerite. It was a big hit with the food truck crowd

31

and I sold out in about two hours. If you have any more of those tomatoes keep them coming. My customers love them. In fact, next time you come, stay a little longer and I will let you try out the dish. If you're really good I might even share the recipe with you.

Alex

She sat staring at her computer screen. Then she read the message again. He had named a dish after her? She felt as though someone special had given her a precious gift. She could feel herself warming. She glanced around even though there was no one in the cottage but the cat who was fully occupied eating and then, as though she were doing a very guilty thing, she clicked on Alexei's website.

Not for the first time.

She felt like an adolescent with a crush but she couldn't help herself. Truth was, she was a grown woman with an adolescent crush! There weren't many pictures of him on the site. Mostly pictures of the food truck, and information on hours and locations. There was a section for reviews and a bit about his philosophy of food. There were only three pictures where Alexei was clearly visible. In her favorite he was leaning out passing a plate of food to a customer. It was clearly not a professional photograph, but whoever had snapped the candid, no doubt a woman, had caught the beauty of Alexei. Marguerite drank him in the way a dying woman might drink from a clear cold stream in the middle of a desert. He was so beautiful. And he loved food the way she did.

A second photo showed him and his truck at a charity event, and the final picture was of him in Greece picking olives with an older man who vaguely resembled him. Obviously a family member. She allowed herself one more long, lingering moment staring at his pictures and then resolutely clicked out of his website. She wondered how many women in the greater Portland area or, for all she knew, women all over the world, indulged themselves in the same way, sneaking peeks at his website. That was the trouble with gorgeous men, everyone wanted them. Nobody knew that better than she did. Timothy had taught her the truth about beautiful men, that they couldn't be trusted.

She responded to all her orders for the week and checked the weather forecast. The rain had worsened, but if the forecast was correct, they'd be harvesting again in three or four days.

She found herself staring blankly at her computer screen. Tomatoes Marguerite! He'd named a dish after her.

Iris was right, she was a woman in her prime. What she should be doing was dating. Not drooling over a man she could never have, but looking for one who would stick around and, even better, might stay faithful.

Dating.

She walked slowly back to her computer and pulled up a website. An online dating website. It wanted her to register right away, but before she committed herself, it did allow her to search. She put in her parameters: age, geographical area, and then she hit the search button. Rows of pictures of men came up. It was like a high school annual from hell. It went on and on and on, page after page of single men.

Marguerite didn't like to rush into things. She let the idea settle the way she'd let a new crop settle. Give it time to root. She mulled over online dating while she attended a meeting on water conservation at the town hall. Her brother, James, the local sheriff was already sitting in the front row when she got there, so she settled beside him. She pushed her wet umbrella into her bag and whispered, "Great timing. A meeting about water conservation during a rain storm."

"Thanks for coming anyway. I might have to leave early in case there's flooding."

She was home from the meeting by eight o'clock and as she flipped on lights in the quiet cottage, she made her decision.

Before she chickened out she picked up her phone and called her sister. "Iris, are you busy?"

"By busy, do you mean wrapped up in cotton wool and not even allowed to put a dish in the dishwasher?"

Not wanting to get into whatever issues Iris was having with an overprotective boyfriend, she said, "Do you think you could come over?"

"Music to my ears. A get-out-of-jail free card." She said it loud enough presumably for Geoff to hear her.

"I need your help with, um, a project."

"If it has anything to do with glue, hot glue guns, wool, or any sort of plant material I am not your girl."

"I know. That would be like you asking me to bake."

"Just so we're clear. What kind of project?"

She pictured Geoff hovering in the background. "I can't talk about it on the phone."

Which made her sound completely crazy. It was like the old days when the Chance home had a party line and old Enid Bailey used to listen in on everyone's conversations. Even though Enid no longer listened to every word, somehow, she could not put the fact that she was contemplating online dating out in the airwaves or phone waves or whatever system carried her voice to some other person's ears miles away. Then she remembered her sister's condition. "I could come to you, if you'd like. Maybe you should be resting with your feet up."

"Honestly, it will be great to get out of this house just so I don't have Geoff fussing over me and telling me to put my feet up every five seconds."

When Iris arrived, she looked suitably curious. "What's up?" Iris asked, as she shook the rain from her jacket before hanging it up.

"You have to promise not to tell anybody."

"Oh, I am so glad I came tonight. I need to stop obsessing about myself and the baby and think about something else for a change. Like you having a secret." She tilted her head sideways. "Wait, I know, you're having wild and crazy sex with that Greek food truck guy, aren't you?"

Marguerite shook her head so hard her curls slapped her. "No. And don't put that image in my head."

"Okay. You don't want to have crazy sex with the hot Adonis food truck guy? Because I have to tell you our mother sure does."

Since Daphne had never looked at another man seriously apart from her husband Marguerite chuckled as she knew she was meant to. "Wait until you see him, *everybody* wants to have sex with him."

As Iris settled on the couch, she said, "Mom seemed to think he had a bit of a crush on you."

Marguerite sat opposite in her comfiest chair. "Come on. Mom thinks everybody loves us as much as she does."

"She's not that bad. Okay, moving on, what's your secret?"

Marguerite took a deep, slow breath. "I'm thinking about online dating."

"Wow. You're seriously taking my advice." She nodded briskly. "This is good. I think it's a really smart idea, you're tucked away out here…"

"I know. Don't give me the Snow White routine again." She shifted uncomfortably. "I tried to make a profile but I can't seem to get started. I thought, you being a real writer, maybe you could help me."

Iris flexed her fingers like a maestro warming up at a Steinway. "I am itching to get started."

"Don't you do anything I wouldn't like. No boasting."

"See, that's why you need me to write your profile. It's a sales pitch. You have to boast." She picked up the laptop from the table between them and Marguerite shifted so she was sitting beside her sister. That earned her a glare. "You're hovering. You're as bad as Geoff! Scoot."

"I'll put the kettle on." She walked into the kitchen reminding herself that she didn't have to post a profile. She could think about it first.

She didn't ask what kind of tea Iris wanted. She took out a few jars from her cupboard and made a special brew. When she set it in front of her sister, Iris glanced at the ruby liquid and said, "What is this? It doesn't contain caffeine does it?"

"No. It's a mixture of dandelion, nettle, ginger and rose hip. It's good for you. It's got lots of vitamins and minerals. Plus the ginger will settle any morning sickness."

Iris opened her eyes in astonishment. "How do you know these things?"

"Because I grow them. Herbs and natural healing are an interest of mine."

"Wow. You're like a shaman." She sipped cautiously. "It's even good."

"I'll send you home with a jar of it." Then she glanced over her sister's shoulder and her eyes widened in horror. "Where did you get that picture of me?"

"I knew you'd have a bunch of boring crap on your own computer so I pulled this off my phone. I love this picture of you. It was taken at Evan and Caitlin's wedding, remember?"

"Of course I remember." She smiled in reminiscence. "That was a great day."

"It was. It seems kind of, I don't know, like we're putting the idea of marriage out there by showing you at a wedding on your profile. Not that you can tell it's a wedding. It's a very subliminal message. And you look gorgeous in that dress."

The gown she'd worn for Evan and Caitlyn's garden wedding was a simple blue dress that left her shoulders bare. Her hair was piled on top of her head and she wore more makeup than usual. "You don't think it's, I don't know, showing me in a way I don't normally look? Like false advertising?"

"No. I don't. Most women would kill for your body. Between the yoga and all that gardening, you look amazing. This is about presenting your assets in the best light."

"I think I prefer to leave my assets in the dark."

They huddled together over the computer. Iris said, "I know this is hard. But it's how everybody meets these days."

Marguerite wasn't so sure. "Lots of people don't meet online, people who go to work and have normal jobs meet each other at work. That's how Rose and Matt met. It's how you and Geoff met."

"Yeah. Or you could ride a big-ass motorcycle

randomly down a country road and meet the love of your life like Evan did."

"Okay, that was kind of random, but you see what I mean? People meet because they're meant to." She frowned. "People who live in big cities have social lives and play sports and things, they don't need to go online to date."

"Yes, yes. Even people who meet other people all the time still date online. It's the way people connect. I mean, think about it. Everybody on here is looking for romance like you are."

"Not everybody. I've heard about people who are just on there for hook-ups."

"I think that with a little bit of common sense you'll be able to figure out which ones are the good guys. Okay, here's where you describe herself. Iris had control of the keyboard which made Marguerite slightly nervous, but she figured she could always change the description later. She said, "Okay, um, I like to garden. I think the world would be a better place if we all tried to get on. I believe in gun-control and—"

"No, no, no." Iris cried. Her hands had yet to move on the keyboard. "If you say you like to garden it makes you sound like an old woman. And as for the rest, you're not running for political office. The whole point of this is to sell yourself as a great potential mate. You have to think about what makes you attractive to a man."

"Are you serious?"

"Of course I am. This is a sales pitch, a marketing tool."

"I want a date not to make employee of the month!"

"Trust me. I think we should write what we think sounds good. We can always run it by Geoff or Evan for a man's opinion."

She grabbed her sister's arm. "No! You have to promise me you won't tell anyone about this. I'd die of embarrassment if anyone knew what I was doing."

Iris looked at her as though she were crazy. "All right. We'll do the best we can." Iris chewed her lower lip for a moment and then she began to type. While Marguerite watched, words formed. Words she would never have written about herself. In the headline box, Iris typed:

Love to See Things Grow

Marguerite stared at the line critically, then nodded. "I like that, it's got two meanings."

Iris grinned at her. "When I'm not baking muffins, I'm a creative writer."

Marguerite hoped Iris didn't have to get too creative to make her sound interesting and desirable.

I've travelled, but I'm more of a homebody. I run a thriving agricultural business which I'm very proud of. I am passionate about good food. I'm loyal, I practice yoga every day to stay in shape, I love being close to nature.

Iris turned to her. "What do you think so far?"

"I think it's pretty good. When you say I'm

passionate about good food, won't people think I can cook?"

"You can cross that bridge when you come to it." She typed, "I speak French. People tell me I'm relaxing to be around." Iris glanced at her. "You are, you know? It's a great quality." She turned back to the keyboard. "Now, here's the fun part. What are you looking for in a man?"

"Oh. I get to make a list?"

"Absolutely. Online dating is all about figuring out what you want and the kind of person you want to be with and then navigating this huge sea of potential partners."

Marguerite thought about what she wanted in a man. Unfortunately, the first image that jumped to her mind was of Alexei, who was basically a fantasy come to life. And who had no connection to her reality. Which was why she was here inventing a dating profile. The pause lengthened as she tried to think of the qualities the mattered most to her. *So good-looking it makes my eyeballs hurt to look at you* was probably not the best thing to put first on her list. While she was thinking Iris began to type. She watched, fascinated, as this woman who knew her so well put together her idea of Marguerite's perfect partner.

I am looking for a man with integrity. If he's like me, he enjoys the simple things in life. A sunrise, a walk on the beach holding hands. I'm a romantic and it would help if you are too.

Marguerite smiled at the words. "Do you see me as a romantic?"

Iris looked at her as though she'd said something incredibly stupid. "Yes! You're completely romantic. You're the only woman I know who, at the end of *Gone With the Wind*, seriously believes Scarlett's going to get Rhett back."

"I do think she'll get him back. I think, in the end, you can't fight true love. Even if you try."

Iris grinned at her. "You see? Total romantic."

"Ha! Look at you. The story of you and Geoff couldn't be more romantic. There you were, looking at potential baby daddies on the Internet, kind of like what we're doing now, and all the time there he was, this sweet, steady man. You tried to fight your attraction even as everyone could see you two falling in love with each other. Are you going to tell me that wasn't meant to be?"

"No. But deep down I'm sort of a corny romantic, too." As Iris's hand slipped to her belly, she said, "Who'd have believed I'd get my fairy tale ending?"

"I did."

"Okay, let's do this thing," Iris said, and before Marguerite was at all ready, her sister pushed a few buttons and said, "There. You're officially signed up on an online dating site."

"Wow. I kind of want to call it back." She suddenly hated her profile photo, thought Iris's description of her was all wrong and mostly wished she'd spent the evening perusing seed catalogues.

"Give it some time. You can always tinker with your profile later. I want that for you, too, you know," Iris said. "The whole fairy tale. There's a wonderful man out there waiting for you."

An icon flashed up indicating she had received her first Internet dating message.

Iris grinned. "Maybe that's him, there. Your fairy tale prince." She pulled her hands away from the keyboard. "You do the honors."

Marguerite clicked on the message feeling a flutter of anticipation she hadn't expected.

Hey there, Cutie. Got any naked pictures? hotforyou78.

Iris sighed. "Even fairy tales have their trolls."

FOUR

"WHAT AM I going to do?" She stared in horror at her sister. The message sat heavy in the air, as though someone had made an off-color joke in church.

Iris reached over. "Watch and learn," and then she pressed the delete key. "And *hotforyou* is no more."

"I'm not sure I'm cut out for this," she wailed.

That earned her a pat on the shoulder. "Maybe give it longer than three minutes before making a final decision on online dating." Then Iris rose. "I need to pee, which is something I'm saying a lot these days. Then let's sit and have some more of this tea, which I wish could be wine."

They sat for ages chatting. Marguerite lost count of the times she saw her sister's hand slip to her belly almost as though she could feel the new baby growing inside her even though, of course, it was far too early.

"Are you thinking you might find time to get married?" Iris and Geoff had been engaged for months. At first, they'd planned to have their wedding in the summer, while Geoff was off school. But somehow the wedding hadn't happened yet. Iris had claimed that opening her second bakery/café kept her too busy to plan a wedding.

Iris put on a fake smile. Marguerite had known her forever and could never remember being treated to it before. "Oh, we'll get to it. But Geoff's so busy with school. Can you believe the Fall Fair is almost here? I feel like we barely got cleaned up from the Fourth of July fireworks! Where does the time go?"

The Chances were not a traditional family, not by anyone's standards. Not even by Oregon's standards. When Daphne and Jack had met in the late 1970s, on a Greyhound bus, nineteen-year-old Daphne had been pregnant. And Jack, who at that point was basically a drifter with a good heart, fell in love with her. Maybe it wasn't anyone's dream to experience passionate romance on a Greyhound bus, but Marguerite had always found the story romantic. Jack and Daphne had come here, to this very property, owned at that time by Daphne's great aunt Mildred who had taken them in. They'd married, as young and ill-equipped as they were. Gone on to build their family. Marguerite sometimes thought of the Chances not so much as a family, but a tribe. Some of the eleven of them were Daphne and Jack's natural children and the rest were strays, picked up along the way.

Jack and Daphne were passionate about many causes, but their main one was that no child of theirs would ever feel inferior to another child. They went so far in refusing to distinguish between their adopted children and their birth children that the kids themselves didn't even know who was who. The older ones had a pretty good idea about the parentage of the younger ones, but it was an unbreakable rule in their house that no one shared their knowledge, either within the walls of the house or outside it.

As far as she could tell, every one of them had honored that rule and been bound by it. The deal in the family was that at sixteen a child could ask. If they wanted to know, Daphne and Jack would tell them as much as they themselves knew about the child's parentage. Iris had discovered she was adopted and taken steps to track down her birth parents. It hadn't been a happy story.

Marguerite had never bothered to ask. She didn't really care. She was as connected to this land as she was to her family. This was home. Maybe when she got to the point, like Iris, where she was going to have a child, she'd want to know about her background. Until then, it wasn't relevant. Jack and Daphne were her parents as much as this place was home.

Iris had always been more concerned about things like parentage. She'd shown strong nurturing instincts from the time she was a child and had always wanted to be a mom herself. Geoff lived in a rental apartment, while Iris owned a pretty house in town with plenty of room to raise a family. So why was Marguerite not being asked to help pack boxes, or lend a hand in moving Geoff in? Why was Iris not even talking about their future together? It didn't make sense.

She rose to more rain. It was too cold this morning to sit outside on her porch, so she set her rocking chair by the window looking out on the garden. Normally, this was her favorite time of the day, as she looked out on her life's work and began to plan her day. But she still felt uneasy.

When Geoff had arrived in Hidden Falls last year he'd brought some emotional baggage with him. He'd come to teach high school in the middle of the year, after his marriage had broken up. When Iris met him he wasn't even divorced yet. At the time, Iris had been skeptical that Geoff was ready to move on but his baggage had turned out to be pretty light. Whatever anger and drama his marital breakup had entailed, she got the sense that his first marriage had been a mistake and in Iris he'd found the woman he'd always dreamed of.

She put herself through her usual morning routine of yoga. As always, the familiar stretches and moves helped calm her, but the tiny niggle of worry about her favorite sister didn't disappear.

She ate a breakfast of eggs, laid by her own hens, and toasted whole-wheat bread that she got from Iris's bakery. For fruit she ate her blueberries and some of the raspberries that were still ripe on the vines.

Then, feeling like she was doing something slightly risqué, she decided to see what was going on in the world of online dating. As she turned on her computer she told herself that if all she got was solicitations for naked pictures that she would delete her profile. She'd gone into this with trepidation anyway, the last thing she needed was extra stress.

However, when she pulled up the site she found that she had several new messages. The first was from a man who sounded very nice, was also a farmer, but sadly lived in another state. He was clearly looking for a farm wife and, while she wished him well, she explained by return message that she had no desire to relocate to Iowa. The second message was from a guy who posed with some sort of motorized vehicle in every one of his pictures. An ATV, a motorcycle, a speedboat, and a truck with the wheels jacked up. She politely declined his offer to "Maybe hit the road with me one day."

Iris had insisted that she be somewhat vague about her geographical location purely as a practical safety measure but the result was that she was getting replies from people pretty far away from Hidden Falls. One guy lived about an hour away from her but she liked his style. In his email he told her how much he liked her profile pictures and that he was a committed vegetarian. His handle was Vegeman. Marguerite tried very hard not to be judgmental about people who ate meat. Most of her family did. Most of her friends did. But she had to admit, since she was a vegetarian herself, that it would be a little easier if she dated someone who shared her food preferences.

She messaged him back telling him a little bit about herself. A little more than was in the profile. One other message made her laugh.

For a woman who digs in the dirt all day, you clean up real nice. I find earthy women fascinating. Tell me more? –Maybesomeday

The man was a little younger than her, and very vague about his profession, if he had any, but his pictures showed him climbing, cycling, and hiking. She decided that a man who could make her laugh first thing in the morning had to have something going for him. She sent him a cheerful message in reply:

You look pretty earthy yourself with all your outdoor activities. As for me, I stay in shape but I'm not sure I could keep up with you. Tell me more...

–Lovetogrow

Maybe she'd stick with the online dating thing for a bit longer.

The site had an area called match-ups that selected profiles supposedly tailor-made for her. She was curious to see what partners a computer would match her up with. Idly, she began scanning through profiles. They ranged from men who were much older than she to men who were barely out of their teens, guys from all over the map. If the things she'd said about herself had led the computer to find these particular matches for her, than either she, or the program, was pretty wacky.

She decided to believe it was the computer. No, she did not want to meet the tattoo artist who listed extreme fighting as his hobby.

She was flipping through her supposed matches, feeling like she was playing an unwanted game of 'hot, not hot' when there was a knock on her front door. To her surprise, her early morning caller was Iris's boyfriend. Her first instinct was concern. Geoff did not call on her in the early hours of the morning. In fact, he'd never been here without Iris. She put a hand to her heart. "Is everything all right with Iris?"

"Yes! Iris is fine," Geoff replied. "Well, I guess she's fine. She's already at work."

He stood there looking guilty, and then said, "I should've called first. Maybe I shouldn't have come at all. I didn't plan to, but I was driving by and I saw your light on. Can I talk to you about something?"

In the year or so that she had known him, Geoff had become almost as close as one of her brothers. She loved him for himself, as well as for the fact that he made Iris so happy. Now that she was sure her sister was okay she smiled at him and opened the door wider.

"Of course. Come on in. Do you want some coffee or something?"

"No. It's okay. I won't stay long. I just … I'm feeling a little troubled and, like I said, I saw your light."

"Then it was a sign you were meant to come here. Sit down and tell me what's on your mind."

He sat on the couch, in the very same spot where Iris had sat last night. Almost as though he felt her presence there. Marguerite knew she was being fanciful but she liked the notion that two people could be so in harmony. Except it seemed they weren't quite so in harmony as she'd believed. Geoff certainly looked as though he was worried and didn't quite know how to begin.

She let him find his way into the conversation, knowing that the best thing she could do for him was simply to listen carefully. She sat across from him in the same place she had sat with Iris last night.

He was dressed for school in black jeans with a check shirt and a skinny tie. He had a tweed jacket thrown over the ensemble. He looked like a sexy, rumpled teacher and she bet a lot of the girls in his class were half in love with him. His face was what she would've called pleasant, comfortable, without being super handsome until he looked at her with those blue eyes and then she could definitely see his appeal. But right now his blue eyes didn't twinkle. He rubbed his face as though he were tired.

Finally he spoke. "Maybe this is out of line, and if it is, I'm sorry. Maybe it's even a betrayal of Iris to talk to you about this, but I know you're her best friend and I'm wondering if you can answer one very simple question for me."

"I'll try." She didn't bother telling him that her first loyalty was to Iris, because he already knew that. There was a beat of silence and then, as though the words were pushed out of him he asked, "Why won't she marry me?"

"Why won't she marry you?" she repeated. Okay, this was a surprise. "Aren't you still engaged?"

He leaned forward and threw up his hands. "Of course we are. But she keeps postponing the date. The day we found out about the baby, we were so happy. Life seemed absolutely perfect. I said something like, 'We should get married before you start showing,' something like that. And she got this panicky look on her face. Like this was a completely new concept she hadn't contemplated before. Then she said it was too much stress with the baby coming."

He suddenly rose to his feet as though he couldn't remain sitting any longer. "Do you mind if I get some water?"

She was tempted to jump to her feet and get it for him but she realized he needed to move, he needed something to do, so she simply said, "Can you bring me one, too?"

In the minute or two that it took him to fetch two glasses of water she had a little time to think. So had he. The first thing he said was, "Maybe I'm not the greatest catch in Oregon, or even Hidden Falls come to that, but we're having a child. We're engaged. Why the hell won't she marry me? Do you think she's having second thoughts about me?"

She could hear the hurt in his voice and was aware of an instinct to soothe, to make things right. Iris had always been the one in the family that everyone went to with their problems. She was the oldest girl and the kind of person who listened as though she really cared, because she did really care about people. Counseling didn't come so naturally to Marguerite, but there was nothing she wouldn't do for the people she loved. She loved Iris and she'd come to love Geoff.

She sipped her water and then said slowly, "I don't understand it, either. I thought maybe you were both too busy to plan a wedding."

He snorted. "I'd go to the town hall and get married on my lunch hour. I don't care about the party, I want Iris as my wife. But when I pressed her, she babbled something about only being able to handle so many huge life changes at once."

"Iris said that? It doesn't sound like her." Iris was a planner, and a doer.

"I didn't think so, either."

"Have you tried to talk to her again?"

"Of course I have. Why do you think I'm here? She tells me she can't think about it right now, or changes the subject." He glanced up at Marguerite and she could see the pain in his face. "I love that woman. I love her so much, I can't imagine how I could go on without her. And we're going to have a baby. I may be old-fashioned, but I think if you love each other and you're about to have a baby, then why the hell wouldn't you get married?"

She answered his unspoken question, because she could hear it clanging loudly around her living room. "I can tell you one thing, Geoff," she said with certainty. "If she's putting off the wedding, it is not because she doesn't love you." She smiled a little. "As you say, we are very close. I have never seen Iris so crazy in love with anyone as she is with you."

"Then why? Why won't she even talk about it? Maybe she wants the next few months to be all about her and the baby, I can understand that. I'll wait. But I need to know." He sat for a moment and repeated, "I need to know."

She sat quietly for a moment, thinking about Iris and letting her intuition consider snatches of conversation, the way Iris was pushing the people she loved most to a distance. Scraps of conversation. Geoff sipped his water and waited as though she were an Oracle and could give him the answers to life's problems.

She thought she understood at least partly what Iris was going through. "My sister has always been fiercely independent. She's the oldest girl and used to taking charge. When you first met her last year she'd given up on finding love and marriage and babies in the traditional way. She was shopping for a sperm donor and hoping she hadn't left it too late. And then you came along and offered her love and marriage and babies in the traditional way. Maybe sometimes, when we get our dreams offered to us, we're too frightened to believe in them. Maybe because, if they don't come true it would break us. So it's easier not to believe."

He was watching her face intently, and nodded slowly. "I know she's scared. It's why she won't tell your mom or anybody until she feels like the risk of miscarriage is really low."

"Maybe, in some strange way, she feels like getting married will jinx the pregnancy or something. I'm making this up as I go along, but it sort of makes sense to me."

"But that's crazy. I'm here for her. I love her! I don't want her to shut me out."

"Maybe you need to tell her that. Don't push the marriage thing. But let her know that you're feeling left out. Iris is always the person people go to with their problems. Present this to her as a problem you're having. I bet she's not seeing how this is affecting you."

He didn't look thrilled with the idea. "You want me to act like one of those whiners who are always wasting her time and getting free therapy?"

"Maybe it's a terrible idea, but it's all I've got. Really, Iris is the one who's so good at solving people's problems."

He rose and headed for the door. "You're not so bad." She followed him. "Don't screw it up this time. I want you for my brother."

He laughed. "I better not. Because I definitely want you for my sister."

FIVE

WHEN SHE CHECKED her messages again that day she found that *Vegeman* had replied.

Do you grow pulses? They use half the nonrenewable energy of most traditional crops. Hardly need any water, either. Vegeman

She was impressed. Instead of mindless flirting, he wanted to talk about growing food. Cool. She replied:

I grow beans and peas. I'm experimenting with lentils, but they grow better in Canada. You're right, though, about the soil and water.

She spent the rest of the day back and forth with him and found that he knew as much as she did about growing healthy food. He was a software engineer but obviously healthy food was his hobby. By the end of the day he said, "I think we have a lot in common. Would you like to meet up sometime?"

Cold dread hit her like a snap frost. It was one thing to indulge in a few messages with a stranger, but did she actually want to show up, face-to-face, and meet him? With all the awkwardness of first-date conversation? For all she knew he might be a vegetarian by day and a cannibal of single women by night.

"Oh, stop it," she said aloud. She had to stop being scared. But, Iris had impressed upon her that she also had to be safe. When she recalled her own words to Geoff about how fear sometimes stopped people doing the things they wanted most she knew she had to take her own advice. So, she sucked in a deep breath. "You can do this," she told herself firmly. She typed back, "Ok, I'd love to. What did you have in mind?"

He replied immediately. "Why don't you pick a place you like pretty much anywhere between Seattle and Portland and I'll make it work."

She liked his confidence, she liked his sense of commitment, and the idea that she was worth driving some distance for. More bonus points for Vegeman.

She messaged him back with the one place she could think of where she'd be completely comfortable and not only safe, but have Iris available to give the guy the once over. Of course, it wouldn't do for him to know that so all she said was, "There's a wonderful café in a little town called Hidden Falls. It's called the Sunflower Coffee and Tea Company. I could meet you there any morning say around 11 AM?"

The mouse clicked and a little electronic whine let her know that her message was sent. She'd done it. She'd agreed to meet and there was no way she could pull that message back. Marguerite wasn't normally a nervous or restless person so when she jumped up from her seat and pushed back as though her computer was about to explode, the cat freaked out and ran past her to make good out the cat door. She wished she could get out of awkward situations as easily. She did the only thing she could think of and phoned Iris who, thankfully, picked up right away.

"Hey, Marguerite, what's up?"

"I'm having a panic attack. I need your help."

Iris laughed. "You would not know what a panic attack is. You live your life in a zone of such peace and tranquility you make the rest of us crazy with jealousy."

"That was before I signed up for on-line dating. It would make anyone crazy."

"Oh no. More naked picture guys?"

"No! Worse! I think I said yes to my first date."

Iris's chuckle was both amused and understanding. "Honey, that's fantastic. Who, what, when, where and why?"

"You sound like you're going to write an article about it."

"I might. Actually, you gave me kind of a fun idea for a short story."

"I'm glad my trauma and panic are useful to someone."

"So? Spill. I want all the details."

"He sounds nice. He's a vegetarian."

At that moment she received a reply to her message. Her voice rose a notch closer to hysteria. "And he's meeting me tomorrow at 11 in your coffee shop."

"Here? Fantastic. I can't believe I didn't think of that myself. Of course, bring all your dates here. I can check them out, make sure they're acceptable to my sister and, if anyone gives you any trouble, I can rally the toddler moms, the seniors with their crossword puzzles, my budding screenwriters, and nobody messes with me or my baristas."

"I hope I'm not making a terrible mistake."

"Relax, it's coffee."

"But what if it's awful? What if we hate each other? What if I can't think of anything to say?"

"I think what you have to do is tell him right up front that you have to be somewhere at noon. 12:15 maybe. Then, if it's the best hour you've ever had, you can check your phone and find out that your meeting got magically cancelled, or you can make another date. But I think it's probably a really good idea to go in with an end time in mind."

"In case he's a serial killer?"

"In case he's boring."

"Or I could cancel the date right now, stay single forever and let my four hundred cats keep me company until the day I die."

"An excellent alternative. I'll see you tomorrow at eleven."

Before she hung up Marguerite said, "Iris?"

"What?"

"Any advice? You've done a lot more dating than I have."

"Relax and be yourself." There was a pause. "And maybe check his picture against the website for America's most wanted."

Alexei and Melissa worked side by side in the food prep area of his Portland food truck. It was peaceful, rhythmic work. Melissa had her earphones in, which he didn't mind her doing as long as he was around to keep an eye out for customers who might show up at this time of day. Her body swayed slightly to the music and he could hear the tinny echo of Tegan and Sara through her headphones.

Since Melissa wasn't interested in talking he was able to let his mind float free while his hands went about the familiar tasks of slicing onions into tiny slivers and preparing the lamb and chicken skewers for the next rush of customers.

He reached up onto the shelf for oregano and saw where he'd pinned his recipe for Tomatoes Marguerite. He paused on the scrap of paper wondering when he'd see Marguerite again. She didn't always bring his produce order herself so he never knew. Marguerite Chance. He had liked her from the first moment they met. At first, she had seemed a little shy around him, but as soon as he got her talking about organic rainbow chard or heirloom squash, her eyes lit up. Her whole person seemed lit up from within. He liked the way her hands moved. They weren't pretty, manicured hands.

They were working hands. The nails were short-tipped and cut bluntly and he knew there'd be calluses on her fingers. She wore a couple of silver rings and they had sparked in the light adding a nice contrast to those very earthy gardener's hands. Then there was her hair. Maybe it was his Greek heritage but he loved a full head of long curly hair on a woman, and Marguerite's was rich and gorgeous.

Trouble was, he couldn't tell if she was interested in him. He was never certain how women really felt about him.

It was, of course, The Curse.

Alexei was enough of a Greek to believe firmly in curses. Most of Greek mythology revolved around all the tricks that fate could play on an unsuspecting mortal. The trick that fate had played on him was giving him the kind of looks that made him attractive to women. His mother had called him Beautiful Boy and his first clear memory was of a woman he didn't know dropping to her knees in front of him when they were at the park, his chubby hand in his mother's. She'd pinched both his cheeks and cried out, "What a perfect little Adonis!"

When he'd been a teenager and too stupid to know better, he'd believed he was pretty hot stuff. Girls used to come onto him all the time, older women who should've known better, and he could barely go out in public without being approached by casting directors, modeling scouts, or rich women looking for a boy toy.

When he tried to complain, his brothers mocked

him. Called him Beautiful Boy just like their mother.

But his physical assets weren't a blessing so much as a curse.

Was that all women wanted? A pretty face? Frankly, some of the things women had said and done – the verbal come-ons, the way they'd touch him -- would have counted as sexual harassment if he were a woman. Not that he'd ever say anything, because he'd sound like an ass, but it was uncomfortable.

He tried everything to downplay his looks. When he went through a spell of dressing like a slob and stopped shaving, he discovered that lots of women went for the unshaven slob thing. His mother had shaken her head at him. "Beautiful Boy. One day you'll be old, maybe fat, and you may wish your perfect beauty back again." But he knew he wouldn't.

In the end, he decided to dress the way he wanted to dress. He wore clothes that were comfortable, mostly jeans and T-shirts. He kept his black curly hair cropped short because that was more practical and he shaved regularly because he didn't like feeling like a slob.

Over time, he'd developed a series of scripts that he pulled out according to need. Modeling scouts, casting agents, anybody want to make a profit from his face got a simple "No, thank you." He refused even to accept business cards. Women who hit on him got a regretful speech about how he was deeply in love with his girlfriend.

The foolish truth was that he hadn't had a

girlfriend in almost a year because the last breakup had been so painful.

There weren't many women he genuinely trusted in his life. There was his mother, his kitchen helper Melissa, and that was about it.

Then he'd met Marguerite, a woman who didn't look at him as though she were picturing him naked in some porn scene she was directing. A woman who, in fact, virtually ignored him until the subject of vegetables came up. He smiled in reminiscence. Since he happened to be interested in food also, he'd made that his excuse to ask for her email. If anything, they had become farmer buddies. Pen-pals who swapped ideas about current growing trends, the 100 mile diet, the Paleo diet. She'd challenged him to use more locally sourced produce and he'd accepted her challenge by buying as many of her organic veggies as he could get.

When she came to see him, it wasn't to ask him out or to flirt with him, it was to bring him glorious fresh bounty. All the women over the years who had made it patently obvious they were available to him, many of whom had outright asked him for dates ranging from coffee to weekends in Paris hadn't moved him at all. And this one, who appealed to him more than any woman had in a long time, didn't seem interested at all.

While he was mulling over the irony of fate, he heard himself hailed by name by a voice he knew all too well. He turned to find his brother Matt, grinning at him through the delivery window. Beside him was Portland's prettiest GP, Dr. Rose Chance. Since his big brother Matt had lost his heart to the sexy doc, he'd become a lot more mellow. Also, since Rose loved his souvlaki platter, his surgeon brother had also become a more frequent customer

"Hey, Bro, what's up?"

"I put in a couple of stents this morning and rebuilt a heart, but other than that not much. You?"

"I chopped about a bushel of cucumber and marinated a lamb. Rose?"

She shrugged her elegant shoulders. "I helped a mother birth a baby."

"Great. You guys brought life into the world and rebuilt hearts today. I chopped vegetables. That kind of puts my life in perspective."

"Does that mean our meals are on the house?" his brother asked hopefully.

He pretended to think about it. "Nah. You're richer than me, too. I feel inadequate enough."

Since she was accustomed to their foolish banter Rose left them to it. But he was happier to see her than usual. It occurred to him that Rose was another woman he could trust. She was in love with his brother and had no interest in him. Plus, while the intimacy between him and his brothers usually meant joking around and fisticuffs, girls were different. Sisters, he'd been reliably informed, told each other secrets.

He started their orders and then, as though the idea had just occurred to him, he said, "I was gonna take a lunch break myself. Okay if I eat with you guys?"

"Absolutely," Rose said, before Matt could say anything stupid.

When the meals were ready, Alex and Melissa carried them out. Matt and Rose had already commandeered the small metal table in front of his truck. Even though he ate his own food most days, he always tasted with a critical palate making sure the flavors were right. Matt ate with the quick efficiency of a surgeon on call. Rose was more relaxed, but he caught her checking her watch once. No doubt she still had patients to see later that day. He knew that if he wanted to get Rose's advice he was going to have to speak up. And fast. Trouble was, he didn't know how to phrase his request for information. Finally, he said, "I saw your sister Marguerite the other day."

Rose glanced up and nodded, waiting for him to go on.

"She brought me some of her produce. Gorgeous heirloom tomatoes."

Once more Rose nodded. "She's got a green thumb, that's for sure." She continued to regard him as though assuming that he had brought up Marguerite and her tomatoes for some reason.

To his intense discomfort, Matt also raised his head and looked at him with the same intensity he probably gave to his patients before he cut into them. "You got some kinda thing for Marguerite and her tomatoes?" Matt finally asked him.

He didn't particularly appreciate the way his

brother phrased it, but he'd pretty much hit the nail on the head, Alex said, "I wouldn't have put it that way, but I like her."

Rose and Matt exchanged a glance that could have meant anything. It was one of those secret glances between couples that was indecipherable to an outsider. Matt spoke again. "You like her as in she's a fun person to hang out with? You can talk about pH levels in the soil and the best way to sauté green pepper? Or you *like her* like her."

"I don't think Marguerite ever sautéed a pepper in her life." He let out his breath, wishing he'd never brought the subject up. But he had, and since he was taking the teasing anyway, he might as well get whatever information they had to share. He glanced at Rose. "Do you know if she's seeing anyone?"

Before Rose could answer, Matt pushed his chair back and laughed, his eyes dancing with unholy amusement. "Wait, wait, wait. You mean, you are interested in a girl and you're not sure if she's interested in *you*?"

Rose smacked her boyfriend in the shoulder. "Would you play nice? Just because you finally got the woman you lusted after for months, you don't need to act smug."

Matt gave her the kind of grin that made Alexei look away in embarrassment. "I did lust after you, didn't I? Fact is, I still do. Probably always will." He shook his head. "But you don't know what it was like growing up in the same house with a guy who looks like that." He pointed his thumb at Alexei. "Girls tried everything to get his interest. They climbed in our windows, asked me to carry notes." He screwed up his face in pain and Alexei was pretty sure he knew what was coming next. "They wrote him poetry. And love songs."

"Would you stop?" But he might as well have asked the sun to stop shining, or the wind to stop blowing, as get his brother to shut up now he was launched into the old stories.

"The best was the tattoo."

Alex shook his head. "No. That was the worst." At least, of the things Matt knew about, that was the worst.

Rose was watching the pair of them as though they were some kind of a comedy duo on a stage. She was a beautiful woman at the best of times but when she was relaxed and smiling, like now, she was a knockout. "Tattoo?"

Matt nodded. He pointed to his own chest with one finger. "Ashley somebody or other, in high school. She had *I love you* tattooed on one breast and *Alexei* on the other. And she liked to wear these really low cut tops."

"I think she got it in Mexico over spring break. Alcohol was definitely involved."

Rose started to laugh. "Oh my gosh, poor Alexei. Did you like her at all?"

He shook his head. He'd felt at the time as though he couldn't get out of high school soon enough.

"I hope she found another Alexei."

He was finally able to see some humor in the situation. "Actually, I saw her a couple years ago. At the beach."

Matt leaned forward. "You get a look at that tattoo?"

He nodded. Grinning.

"She still has it?"

"She had it modified. Now it says, I love you Ashley."

They all laughed. Rose said, "Self-love is good. Hopefully this time she won't get rejected."

Matt said, "So, anyway, back to you and Marguerite. Are you telling me she's not showing any of the signs of being smitten with you?"

"I don't know. We're like pen-pals. We email about veggies and stuff. And when I'm close to her, she sort of acts distant. Uninterested."

"Well, that's a first."

"You don't have to sound so happy about it."

Matt spoke to Rose. "In his whole life he's never once been rejected. Never even had to work up the nerve to ask a girl out. They did all the asking. You know what my Mom's nickname for me is?"

Rose shook her head.

"Big Mouth. You know what she calls Alexei?"

She shook her head again.

"Beautiful Boy!"

Rose patted her lips with a napkin. Then she said, "Well, he is."

"You see?" Matt threw up his hands. "Even my

own girlfriend thinks you're hot."

"Mattius!" she said in a warning tone that sounded scarily like their mom, without the heavy Greek accent.

"Okay, okay. You want us to find out if she's got a guy?"

What he wanted was to find out if he had any hope at all with the sexy organic farmer, but he supposed it would help to find out she was actually single. "Yeah. That would be great."

His cell phone rang and he glanced at it, planning to ignore the call, but when he saw the name Chance he pressed *Talk* all too eagerly. "Alexei speaking," he said. How weird that Marguerite would call him now of all times, when he'd just been talking about her. Maybe his luck was starting to change.

Then a very not Marguerite voice said, "Alexei. It's Daphne Chance. Rose's mother. Have you got a minute?"

"Uh, yes, sure. What can I do for you Mrs. Chance?"

That got Rose's attention, and even Matt stopped chewing to stare.

"Oh, please, anyone who cooks like you do can call me Daphne. And it's about your cooking that I'm calling."

When he got off the phone, his two eager spectators said in unison, "Well?"

"That was your Mom," he said to Rose. "She wants me to bring my food truck to the Hidden Falls

Harvest Festival in two weeks time."

Rose narrowed her gaze on his face as though she were trying to diagnose him with some hitherto unknown disease. Then she nodded. "She's trying to set you up with Marguerite. That's got to be it."

Matt stared at her. "You don't think she wants some souvlaki and spanakopita at the fall fair?"

"Not nearly as much as she wants to get your brother together with my sister. Remember when she dragged us all down here to Alexei's and had told you to meet us without bothering to let me know?"

Matt nodded, his eyes twinkling. "She knew you lusted after me."

"She was matchmaking. Then when Alex and Marguerite started bonding over dandelion greens I saw her eyeballs get the swirling whirligig look. You know, like the wheel of death, right before your computer crashes? It means she wants to get you and my sister together. I'm sure of it."

Alexei let out a slow, breath. "I am crazy about your mother."

"Yes," Matt pointed out, "But we don't know that Marguerite is crazy about you." He looked quite pleased by the idea.

"Well," Rose said, looking from under her lashes at Matt, "we can find out when we head down to Hidden Falls to attend the fair and see my family."

Matt stared at her. "What's this *we*?"

"Iris asked me to come down for a visit. And Mom's the chair of the Fall Fair Harvest Fair

Committee, God help Hidden Falls, and she's planned one of her big family dinners. You know the way she loves a big family dinner. I was hoping you'd come with me."

Matt shrugged. A man who can see that arguing is a waste of time. He said, "Well, at least I'll be able to check out my little brother's crush and see if there's any hope."

"Rose," he appealed, "think of me not as Matt's brother, but as the man who works hard to make you the best lamb souvlaki platter you have ever eaten. Don't let him screw things up, and if you can find out anything about what she thinks of me? I'd really appreciate it."

She nodded. "I'll do my best."

He gathered the empty plates together as the two doctors stood up to leave. Matt said, "Lunch was extra tasty today. Watching my brother squirm somehow added to the flavor."

"I'll add it to your tab."

SIX

MARGUERITE TRIED NOT to feel nervous when she walked into Sunflower at 11 o'clock in the morning. The cheerful chimes welcomed her as did the familiar scents of coffee and fresh-baked bread and bakery goodies. Even though she'd spent an extra half hour meditating this morning her stomach was jumpy.

She glanced around the coffee shop and immediately spotted her date. Her first fear, or maybe it was really a secret hope, was that she might have been stood up. But no, a man who looked very much like his profile photograph sat alone at a table by a window, his gaze fixed on her. She approached the table. "Phil?" she asked softly.

He nodded, then rose and as she was about to extend her hand in greeting he pulled her in for an awkward hug.

"I hope I didn't keep you waiting?" she asked politely. In fact, she had waited around the corner until a few seconds before eleven so as not to appear too eager. She knew she had been exactly on time.

"No. You walked in the door right at eleven."

Well, their watches were in sync, they had that much in common. Phil hadn't smiled in his profile picture, and he didn't smile now. He had a pleasant face, though. Not arresting, or particularly good looking. Not a man who drew a woman's gaze and held it captive. Phil wore a knitted cap that he didn't take off, so she assumed he was probably bald. He had hazel eyes in a pale face, a sharp nose and that unsmiling mouth. When he'd hugged her she had noticed that he was thin, even a little bony, but all in all, nothing about him repelled her. That had to be good.

She had no idea what the etiquette was over a coffee date. Did he pay? Did she? Did they pay for their own? He didn't have anything in front of him so clearly he'd waited for her before ordering. She glanced over to the counter and saw that her sister was making a pretty decent study of her date without appearing to. She was about to suggest they walk up to the counter and check out the baked goods, when, to her surprise, Iris walked over to the table.

"Hello," she said. "It's not too busy right now, so I can take your order right from here if you like." Marguerite had never been so grateful to her sister for making this first date a little bit easier, though she had a pretty strong idea that Iris had wanted to get a closer look at Phil.

She smiled at Iris the way she hoped she'd smile at a stranger and said, "Could I have some green tea please?"

"Sure thing. Would you like a muffin or cookie or anything with that?"

She'd love one of Iris's homemade muffins as her sister must know, but the whole weirdness about who was going to pay for this drink was bad enough without the added burden of muffin costs messing up the already awkward atmosphere so she shook her head.

Her date said, "Do you have anything that's lactose free, gluten free, and vegan?"

"I do a chocolate beet brownie that's vegan. It's lactose and gluten free."

While Marguerite was marveling that her sister could pull out a baked good that met all those criteria he asked, wrinkling his brow, "Is it made with real chocolate or carob?"

Iris didn't look at Marguerite nor did she roll her eyes, but Marguerite could almost see the effort on her eye muscles to hold her eyeball still as she said, "It's made with chocolate."

"I'll just have hot water."

"Coming right up."

Marguerite smiled at him, "I have a lunch meeting at noon."

He nodded. Then spent the next fifty-five minutes lecturing her about environmental degradation and telling her about his food intolerances, his allergies, and his lifelong battle with irritable bowel syndrome.

She made a big production out of leaving at five

minutes to noon, this time making sure to shake his hand before exiting. She hid around the corner until she saw him get into a truck and drive it away. Then she snuck back to the Sunflower Café. When she walked in Iris said, "Oh you poor thing. Do you want another tea?"

She shook her head. "I'm going to need something a lot stronger. Give me a coffee."

Iris's brows rose. "Coffee? You hardly ever drink coffee."

"I know. You'd better make it a double."

"Belly up to the bar, Sister. Coming right up."

After she brought the coffee over to their favorite table, she said, "So, Vegeman…?"

"Let's just say I know more about his bowels than I ever want to. Oh, and when he said that people who eat meat should be threaded onto a spit and roasted over their own gas barbecues I don't think he was being witty." She took a slug of coffee. "One good thing, my day can't get any worse."

Iris glanced up as the Sunflower chimes jingled. "Don't be too sure" she said, as their mom walked in.

She stared at her sister. "You promised you wouldn't tell her about my date," she whispered.

"I didn't!" Iris whispered back. Then she turned to their mother. "Mom! What brings you to this part of town?"

From her large bag, Daphne pulled out a basket. One of Iris's. "I'm returning the basket, from the Fall Fair Committee meeting. Everyone loved your muffins and cookies and I thought Harold Wilson would fall into a diabetic coma after he scarfed most of the lemon bars. There wasn't a crumb left. I felt very proud."

"You didn't have to make a special trip to bring back the basket."

"I had some errands to run and I was happy to have an excuse to pop in and see how you are. I thought you looked a little pale the other day. You're not coming down with something, are you?"

Iris's color deepened and Marguerite could tell that it made her very uncomfortable not to tell Daphne about her pregnancy. There was a tiny pause as though she were debating whether to do just that and then she said, "No. I feel fine."

But Daphne hadn't raised eleven kids for nothing. She had a weird extra sense like a divining rod for lies. While Iris hadn't exactly lied, she hadn't told the whole truth. However, Daphne didn't push the issue, and simply said, "Let me know if there's anything I can do."

"I will. Can I get you a tea or coffee or something?"

"I don't want to interrupt you girls if you're talking about something important."

"No," Marguerite said. "I needed some things at the health food store and decided to drop by."

"All right then, I'd love to join you. I'll have a coffee, too." Iris topped up all their coffees. If Daphne noticed that she poured herself a decaf, she didn't say anything.

"Well, the meeting for the fall fair committee went very well. You know I didn't want to chair the committee this year, but if I hadn't done it we might not have had a fair, and we need the money it raises to keep the after school program going for kids in need."

Daphne had been helping children in need from the moment she stopped being a child herself. They both dutifully made supportive noises.

"Anyway, the one good thing about being the chair is that people tend to go along with my vision. I am determined to make the fair bigger this year, and add some new attractions. We're going to advertise a little farther outside our own community. Lots of people from big cities want to experience a small town fall fair, so why shouldn't we take their money? We'll have the craft fair and of course the booths selling local produce. I've put Paisley in charge of games for the children. Then there's—"

"Paisley's coming home?" Iris interrupted. Paisley was their youngest sister who lived away at university. Paisley was the beauty of the family. If she were a flower, Marguerite thought she'd be an heirloom rose. Perfect to look at, with a divine scent, but more fragile than her hybrid cousins.

"I haven't asked her yet, but she's got a break then and it's time she came home."

"Can't argue with that."

"Where was I," Daphne continued, her mind already off her youngest child and back in her role as chair of the Fall Harvest Fair. "Games for children, oh yes, and for the first time ever we're going to bring in some food trucks."

Marguerite choked on her coffee as horror and dread warred in her belly. Surely her mother hadn't... "Food trucks?"

"Yes." Daphne nodded, her blue-green eyes twinkling. "I asked Alexei first, and he seemed very enthusiastic about the idea. He put me in touch with some other truck owners and I think we're going to have about four or five food trucks, right here in Hidden Falls. Isn't that wonderful?"

Wonderful wasn't quite the term Marguerite would have used. In fact she felt as though someone had sandpapered her esophagus. "You asked Alexei Vasilopoulos to bring his food truck here? To our fall fair?"

"Yes! He's going to try to get his brother Matt as his helper. With the two of them serving food, the women of Oregon will be lining up for miles."

Iris said, "Matt, the cardiothoracic surgeon, is going to help out in a food truck?"

"Sure! He and Rose will come down anyway for the fair and I think he'd get a kick out of it. He told me once that he paid his way through college by working in Greek restaurants. He probably misses it."

Matthew Vasilopoulos was a gifted surgeon who had saved their father's life, along with who knew how many other patients over the years. He was wealthy, busy, and currently dating their GP sister Rose. He did not seem like a guy who would enjoy spending a day slinging souvlaki at a country fair.

"This I've got to see," Iris said.

Marguerite could only be grateful that she'd be running her own produce stand and way too busy to watch the lineup of eager women who wanted to taste Alexei's wares.

A sound like a doorbell ringing emerged from Daphne's bag. She dug out her cell phone and checked her text messages. "That's Jack. He's finished at his doctor's appointment. I'm going to go pick him up now. Thanks for the coffee, darling."

"You're welcome."

Marguerite waited until her mother had shut the door of the coffee shop before thrusting her hands into her hair. "She asked Alexei to bring his food truck to our fall fair? Did I actually hear that right or did I suffer a brain aneurysm thanks to this coffee?"

Iris looked sympathetic. "I'm pretty sure you heard correctly."

"She's trying to set me up, isn't she?"

Iris chuckled. "Of course she is. You have to feel a little sorry for her. After raising eleven kids for all these years, now she doesn't have enough to do. She's taken to matchmaking."

"We really need to nip that in the bud." She glanced over at her sister significantly. "What she needs in her life is a new kid to fuss over. Like, say, a grandchild."

Iris dropped her gaze and began to trace the handle of her coffee mug. "I'm not ready to tell her yet. If anything goes wrong..."

Marguerite reached out and put her hand over her sister's. "If anything goes wrong, who would you want by your side more than Daphne Chance?"

Her sister drew in a quick breath. "I'm so scared. Do you have any idea what it's like to want something so much that the idea of getting it is almost too frightening? Like you somehow don't deserve it?"

She said, "I've never been the one that people come to for advice. That's always been you. There's something about you that makes people want to unburden all their problems and put them on your shoulders. And there's something in you that makes you a really good listener and somebody who gives very good advice. So, I want to try something. I want you to imagine that I'm the one in your position. What advice would you give me?"

But Iris didn't look wise or calm or at all like a person who had all the answers. She shook her head quickly. "I can't see straight. I think it's the pregnancy hormones. My emotions are a mess, I want to sleep all the time, and if I even think about green beans I start to feel sick."

Marguerite couldn't stop the spurt of laughter. "Green beans? Are you serious?"

"As serious as morning sickness." Iris put a hand over her eyes. "Please, don't even say those words."

"I'm so sorry."

"This is going to sound so weird, but I feel like I'm not ready. I'm panicking all the time. Dosana is really busy with the other bakery, and the only other help I have is some kids from the high school who work part-time. Geoff will be able to help next summer, but it's a long time until next summer. I can't do it all. I need a bakery assistant, but I've put the word out quietly and I'm getting nothing back."

"Okay, let's take this one step at a time. I think Mom could use a little more in her life. What about asking her to help out?"

"Then I'll have to tell her why. And I'm not ready."

The conversation she'd had with Geoff yesterday morning was still very fresh in her mind. She had a feeling that Iris was in her stubborn mood where she didn't want to lean on anyone, not even the people closest to her. So she said, quite bluntly, "Why not?"

"I can't even explain it. After I get my scan maybe if I can see that there really is a little baby inside me it will make me feel like this is more real. Mom said Rose is coming down for the Fall Fair. I'm going to tell her, and get her advice on what I should do about running the bakery café and staying healthy."

"That's a really good idea, Rose deals with crazy pregnant ladies all the time. Plus, she's your sister and she loves you. I'm sorry if I've been too pushy."

"No. You haven't. I'm not myself."

"Is Geoff going with you to the scan?"

"Are you kidding me? I'd have to hire thugs to keep that man away."

"That's good. It must be really nice to have the

man you love at your side while you go through this."

She nodded and closed her eyes briefly. "I'm being really hard on him right now too. I don't want to be. I just can't seem to help it."

Marguerite stood up. Maybe Iris needed some time to work out why she was refusing to ask for help from the people who loved her most. "Thanks for the coffee, Iris. I should get going. I have to rush back home to see if any more exciting dates are waiting for me."

The shadows in Iris's eyes disappeared as they began to dance. "All I can say is, the dates can only get better from here."

"I hope you're right."

SEVEN

WHEN SHE GOT home, she discovered that *Maybesomeday* had messaged her. He messaged her most days, often telling her about an epic hike he'd done or a wicked bike ride. He seemed like life was a daily adventure. She bet he didn't talk about his colon on a date.

He said,

Farmer's Almanac says weather will be fair tomorrow.

I thought I'd take an easy bike ride. Want to ride along? –Maybesomeday

She was tempted to refuse, but he seemed nice and it would be good to have a palate cleanser after *Vegeman*. Not wishing to get into another awkward situation regarding food, she replied:

Love to. Why don't I bring a picnic lunch?

To which he replied: *Sweet!*

When she pulled into their meeting spot in her dusty, red truck, he was waiting. He wore baggy shorts and sneakers with a shirt advertising a band she'd never heard of. His hair was blond and curly and he had the kind of too-good-to-be-true innocent blue eyes that reminded her of her younger brother, Cooper's.

When she climbed out of the truck, he said, "Hi Margaret, I'm Chuck."

"It's Marguerite. It's French."

"Right. Okay." He hefted her old mountain bike out of the back inspecting it critically. She didn't know much about bikes but his was obviously a lot newer and fancier. She fetched her helmet and the backpack containing their picnic from her truck. He reached for the backpack and told her he would carry it. She wondered if he was being helpful or afraid she'd fall off her bike and ruin his lunch. Probably a bit of both.

She wore cropped yoga leggings, a hiking shirt and sneakers. In her pack was a light biking jacket in case the weather turned. "Do you have a route in mind?"

"Thought we'd take it easy and ride on the path by the river."

"Sounds good," she said, pulling on her helmet.

And it was good. He went at a reasonable pace and she had no trouble keeping up. After a couple of hours, he pulled over into a clearing beside a large pool. As they dismounted, he said, "I thought we'd eat here."

"Great." She unpacked sandwiches. "I forgot to ask you what you like, so I made hummus and spinach and cheese and tomato."

"Good stuff."

"And there are brownies for dessert."

They chatted over their lunch and he was an easy companion. As she'd suspected, he was underemployed. "I work in a bike shop, part time. I'm kind of finishing my degree in Outdoor Rec. I'm living with my Mom for a while until I get on my feet, you know?"

"I do."

He was only two years younger than she was but seemed a lot younger somehow.

When they got back to her truck he said, "That was fun. Want to do it again sometime?"

She hesitated. He was a nice guy but not for her. She took her time stowing the backpack into her truck and turned back to him. "I would. But could we just be friends?"

"Absolutely. Next time I'll bring the food." And he grinned in a cheerful way and leaned in to kiss her on the cheek.

"Honestly," she said later to Iris, "I think I made a new friend."

"Plus, he ate actual food and didn't tell you about his digestive troubles."

"So, one bad date, one fun friend date so far."

"You know what they say, third time lucky."

The Fall Harvest Fair was a big deal in the limited social calendar of Hidden Falls community events. This being October in the Pacific Northwest, Daphne's biggest fear was rain. Since Marguerite was going to be operating her fruit and vegetable stand, rain had been a big concern for her, also. There were backup plans of course, mostly involving moving a lot of the fair into the high school, but fortunately, contingency plans would not be needed as Marguerite could see from the moment she got up in the morning that the sky was clear.

Marguerite dressed in a pair of jeans and a denim shirt suitable for manning a produce stand. But anyone who knew her well and looked closely would have noticed that she had taken more time than usual with her hair and had even gone so far as to dabble with eyeliner, darken her eyelashes with mascara and swipe clear lip gloss over her lips.

Not that she was dressing up or trying to make herself pretty for anyone in particular.

In spite of the fact that all the proceeds were for charity, she had decided to hire a helper for the day. She knew from past events that the first couple of hours would be very busy, and most of her best stuff would sell out fast.

She arrived early at the fairgrounds. The first person she saw was her brother James, conspicuous in his sheriff's uniform. He caught up with her as she was manhandling a crate of pumpkins out of the back of her truck and hefted them right out of her hands. "I can manage," she protested.

"I know you can. But I need to flex my muscles and look manly or the chicks won't dig me."

She relinquished the pumpkins and grabbed a box

of zucchini and another of onions. James's problem seemed to be the opposite of hers. Since he'd moved back to Hidden Falls to take over as sheriff, he'd become a person of interest to most of the single women in the area. "You expecting much trouble today?"

"Honestly, my biggest worry is overflow parking." James had formerly been a homicide detective in Seattle but surprisingly he'd chosen to become sheriff of Hidden Falls when the post became available. She suspected he'd become a little burned out on violent crime so the slower pace of life suited him, and Hidden Falls was very lucky to have him.

"Have you seen Mom?"

"Would that be the bossy-looking woman with a megaphone?"

She nearly dropped her zucchini. "Someone gave that woman a megaphone?"

"I may have to confiscate it in the interest of keeping the peace."

Other trucks were arriving. She recognized some of the craft fair sellers, the woman who made the most incredible soaps and body lotions using all natural ingredients, a man who carved animals, bowls and small furniture out of wood, a truck advertising grass fed beef, and then Iris's van, painted with sunflowers and advertising the Sunflower Coffee and Tea Company, rumbled into the lot.

After waving to Iris and Geoff, she headed for her usual spot to set up, James in tow, and discovered that her produce stand had been moved this year. She was in a more central location, which was fine. She found herself beside the stall selling homemade soaps and bath salts and various oils. On her other side was a local jeweler and silversmith. The silver winked in the sun as the woman laid out her wares on black velvet trays. Marguerite made a mental note to check out the gleaming jewelry when she had a spare moment.

Her helper, Lefty, was a burly man big in muscle and small in conversation, so they worked mainly in silence while setting up. She was arranging her sunchokes when she heard the sound of a truck approaching. She glanced up and caught the blue and yellow colors of Alexei's food truck. He slowed as he approached and then, to her horror, pulled in exactly across from her produce stand.

He jumped out of the truck looking breathtaking in jeans and a casual shirt. Dark sunglasses covered his eyes. He looked more like a movie star playing the part of a food truck guy than an actual chef. He spoke to someone in the passenger side of the truck who passed him out the printed map of the fair. He nodded, glanced around and then caught sight of Marguerite standing there with a sunchoke in her hand. He pulled up his dark glasses and swaggered over. When he gave her the full wattage of his I-come-from-a-long-line-of-Greek-gods grin, she felt her knees go weak. "Morning. Great day for a fall fair."

She had to force her tongue to work. All it really wanted to do was hang out of her mouth stupidly. "It is." She managed. "It really is a beautiful day."

He made a gesture between his food truck and her produce stand. "Looks like we're neighbors. It'll be nice for me to look over and see a friendly face."

She thought that when the local women started turning up he'd have a long line of very friendly faces to look at but kept that opinion to herself. She said, "I hope you won't be bored. I'm not sure what my mother told you, but this is a small town fair. You might not get a lot of business."

He shrugged his strong, beautiful shoulders. "That's okay. It's nice to do something different. Besides, the money goes to a good cause."

For a second their gazes connected and she was so worried that she was giving away the depth of her embarrassing crush that she immediately looked away. He stood there for another second in silence and then said, "Well, I'll catch up with you later."

"Yes. Later."

Once he turned she allowed her head to rise so she could hungrily watch him walk back to his truck.

Her prediction that Alexei might not get too much action at his truck was quickly proved to be wrong. Maybe it was the good weather, maybe all the extra advertising that Daphne and her committee had organized, or maybe in one of those mysterious ways of the country, word had just spread. Whatever the cause, it was soon clear that this was going to be the best fall fair in Hidden Falls memory. If the lineup for Alexei's food truck wasn't entirely made up of attractive, hungry women, there were enough of those that when she wasn't super busy herself, Marguerite had time to look across and watch beauty at work.

He had a grin and a cheerful word for everybody as he and his assistant, the eminent cardiothoracic surgeon Dr. Matthew Vasilopoulos, turned out steaming meals at an astonishing rate. It might've been a long time since Matthew had worked in a Greek restaurant, but he clearly hadn't forgotten how.

Every once in a while, she'd catch Alexei looking her way and they'd wave.

As she was staring at the pair of them, a voice at her elbow said, "It's enough to make anybody drool, isn't it?" She glanced over to find Daphne following her gaze. "One Greek God turning up in Hidden Falls, Oregon, is amazing enough, but two of them? At our fall fair? And they bring food?"

Marguerite couldn't help but laugh. "Does Dad know about this inappropriate obsession you have with two much younger men?"

"Honey, your dad doesn't have a single gay bone in his body, but he took one look at those two and he completely understood."

As though they somehow knew they were being talked about, the two Vasilopoulos brothers looked up at the same moment and shot the women identical lady-killer grins. Well, identical except that Alexei's was just that tiny bit more breathtaking.

Daphne raised her megaphone to her lips and yelled, "Great job, boys!"

After jumping about a foot, both men waved back. She dragged the megaphone hand down to prevent any further bellowing and said, "The fair's a huge success, Mom. I've never seen so many people here. Congratulations. You did a great job."

"Thanks, I'm so happy it all worked out. The weather turned out perfect!" Then Daphne jerked as though she'd received an electric shock. "There's a reporter from Seattle with a camera crew. I sent out press releases, but I never imagined..." She used a hand to check that her hair was in place and then strode forward.

"Go get em, Mom," Marguerite called after her.

She was bagging potatoes and carrots for a woman who was telling her how lucky she was to live in such a 'darling little town,' when she glanced up to see Chuck standing in line.

When she'd taken the 'darling' woman's money, she turned to say, "Hi. This is a surprise."

"Hi yourself. I thought I'd check out the fair. You made it sound like a lot of fun. And it is." He perused her wares. "Got any apples?"

"Sold out first thing. I can give you a carrot."

"Okay. How much?"

She handed it to him. "On the house."

"So, this is your town."

"It is."

"There's some good hiking around here. We should hit the hills."

"Sure."

Two people stood ready to pay, so he said, "I'll text you. Thanks for the carrot." And he leaned forward to kiss her cheek.

As she said, "You're welcome," she glanced up and found Alexei watching her. He'd no doubt seen the kiss. She waved. Maybe it was childish, but she wanted him to know he wasn't the only one getting attention from the opposite sex.

She managed to escape for a few minutes around two in the afternoon and strolled through the fair stretching her legs. Paisley was doing a brisk trade at the face painting tent, though it was obvious that some of the young men lining up were a lot more interested in Paisley than in having a fanciful animal or star painted on their face. Paisley was the youngest and prettiest of the Chance girls.

Even with the black-rimmed smart-girl glasses she'd taken to wearing, she only looked more adorable. "Hey, Kiddo, how's it going?"

Paisley looked slightly worried. "I'm not artistic. I warned Mom, but you know how she is. I'm okay with the rainbows and stars but some kid asked me to paint a cat on her face and I think it looks like I put the sign of the devil on her."

"I'm sure it will be fine. And remember, the paint washes off."

A small boy approached and sat on the face painting seat. "Do you want a star?" Paisley asked hopefully.

"No."

"Maybe a rainbow?"

"Can I have a dragon?"

"A dragon, um…"

Marguerite leaned in. "Just do another devil cat. And put some red flames coming out of its mouth. It'll be great."

Geoff was front and center at the Sunflower booth and she was happy to see that Iris was sitting on a lawn chair sipping something from a cup. She waved as she went by. It seemed her Mom had roped all of her kids into helping, or all the ones who were around. To her delight she saw her oldest brother Evan helping their youngest brother Cooper with the kids' games. Even Prescott, the world-famous architect had turned up. She suspected he was supposed to be a floater since he wore a fluorescent green vest. He was on his knees in front of Edith May Tittlebury, which made her stop for a moment. Not that she had any intention of rescuing him. Edith May was the worst busybody in Hidden Falls and the way her eyes were flashing and her beaky nose was bobbing up and down like she was hunting for worms, she was either interrogating Scott about his own life or, more likely, letting him in on all the gossip in town that he couldn't have cared less about.

Her stand sold knitting and crochet items that she worked by hand. Everything from frilled toilet roll covers to potholders knitted in the stars and stripes covered her table. There were doilies and socks and an entire section of knitted baby clothes. Marguerite itched to buy something small for Iris but of course

93

she'd never get away without an interrogation about who it was for, and she wasn't a good enough liar to get past Edith May. Prescott had somehow got roped into holding a skein of knitting wool while she rolled it into a ball, though it was obvious that she was talking a lot more than she was rolling.

As she snuck past, she heard Edith May say, "Of course, I don't like to speak ill of the less fortunate, but what was she thinking letting that low life ex of hers borrow her car?" She tsked. "I told your brother James about it and you know what he said?"

"I can't imagine," said in a flat tone.

"He said that the law can help a person if their car is stolen, not if they lend it of their own free will. I tell you, young man, the laws are too forgiving, that's what. And there she is, having to ride her bicycle to work. I see her, every day, when she goes past my house…"

The gossip was drowned by a sudden tinkling sound and she glanced up to see Harold Beidleman had set all his wind chimes ringing. He beamed at her as she walked closer. Harold was an older gentleman somewhere over seventy and probably under a hundred who'd recently moved to Hidden Falls from the East Coast. "That got your attention," he said looking pleased.

"Sure did." She watched as the chimes danced and clashed. One was made with an upside down colander hung with antique cutlery, some were made with sea shells, and one with old keys. "These are beautiful.

Did you make them?"

"Absolutely. Keeps me out of trouble. I get lots of ideas from the Internet. I like Pinterest. And Etsy. My daughter set me up with my own site but it's more fun to sell in person. I've already made eighty-five dollars today." He leaned forward and dropped his voice. "Ripped off the townies, but I figure it's for a good cause, and they can afford it."

"That's great." A pair of strangers in matching Hunter boots and designer sweaters walked up and inspected a wind chime hung with driftwood and broken pieces of jewelry. Obviously they were what he termed townies. She nodded in their direction and winked. "Keep up the good work."

As she walked away, she heard him say, "Allow me to demonstrate," and a delicate tinkling sound followed her.

As she headed back, she threaded her way through kids eating caramel apples, past neighbors and strangers carrying bags filled with their purchases.

Over in the entertainment area, the Hidden Falls Fiddlers were giving a rousing rendition of Louisiana Saturday Night to a small crowd who were clapping and stamping along in time to the music. From the laughter, crowds and the general feeling of goodwill she had to conclude that this year's fair was a roaring success.

Around four things were winding down. All she had left were a few potatoes, two dented onions, and three sunflowers that had somehow been separated from their bouquet. She and Lefty were stacking crates ready to return them to the truck when the sexiest voice in the world called her name softly. She turned and Alexei stood in front of her holding something that smelled delicious in one of his blue-and-white napkins. To her amazement, he offered the napkin-wrapped food to her. "I didn't see you eat anything all day. I thought you might be hungry. This is my vegetarian souvlaki."

She hadn't stopped to think that she was hungry.

And now that she had a moment to think about it she was starving. And charmed by his thoughtfulness. To have noticed that she hadn't eaten anything, he had to have been sneaking glances her way as she'd been doing to him. But she wouldn't even let herself think about that, only about the wonderful smell under her nose. She accepted the offering and allowed herself to be charmed. "You brought me food."

"I would have brought flowers but when a woman's hungry, I think it's better to feed her. Besides," he gestured to the three bright yellow sunflowers, "You already have flowers."

"Thank you." She bit into the souvlaki and her tongue nearly wept for joy. "Mmm. Mmmmm. That is delicious. I didn't know you made a vegetarian souvlaki." The couple of times she'd eaten at his food truck she'd had Greek salad and spinach pie.

"It's new on the menu. I'm trying it out to see how it goes. Lots of vegetarians in Portland." He grinned at her, "And a few in Hidden Falls."

"I guess you'll be heading back soon," she said, and then could have kicked herself for sounding like she cared what he was doing on a Saturday night.

He glanced at her in surprise. "Actually, your mom invited me for dinner. I assumed you knew."

Of course she would have. He was Matt's brother. Somehow, Marguerite hadn't thought it through. And her mom hadn't bothered to mention it. "Oh, right. I wasn't sure you could make it." Which sounded lame.

"I'm looking forward to it." He had such a wonderful voice. Low and sexy.

"Don't get your hopes up. It won't be gourmet! My mom gets so carried away. You'd think she'd be exhausted from running this whole fair, but somehow she'll get dinner on the table for twenty people. She's amazing."

"She is amazing," he agreed. "I think your whole family is amazing." She was munching happily on her vegetarian souvlaki so wasn't compelled to answer him. S;he thought her family was pretty amazing too. The strong and silent Lefty returned and hefted the load of crates that Marguerite had intended to carry to the truck herself. He didn't seem to mind, so she let him go. It was so nice to have Alexei to herself just for these couple of minutes. He seemed in no hurry to leave. After a moment he said, "Before it gets dark, I was wondering if you'd show me your beds."

Her eyes nearly bugged out of her head. "You want me to show you my bed?"

His amusement lit up his whole face. "I mean the

beds where you grow your vegetables."

"Right. *Those* beds." Of course he wasn't interested in her bed. What was the matter with her? She popped the last of the souvlaki into her mouth, scrunched up the napkin, and pushed it into a nearby trash bin. "I'd be happy to."

He turned and shouted across the lane to his brother: "Hey, Matt, you're on cleanup. Marguerite is going to show me her organic gardening set up before it gets dark."

"You owe me," Matt yelled back, but he actually seemed pretty cheerful about being left to hang out in the food truck. She got the feeling it was a nice change from his usual profession. They walked toward her truck and he said, "Okay if you drive? The only wheels I have are back there."

"Of course. It's not that far."

As they walked across the field to where she was parked, the sounds of Annie and Bill Arden singing Islands in the Stream floated over. "They're pretty good," Alex said.

"They should be. They practice it enough. Every birthday party, wedding, anniversary, really pretty much anytime more than five people in town get together, they'll perform." She shrugged. "One of the downsides of small town life."

"I like your town."

She glanced at him. "You do? I thought you were more the big city type."

He thought about it for a moment. "I don't think

I'm any type. I like cities, sure, but I like small towns, too."

They arrived at truck, originally red, now faded by sun and years of driving on dirt roads. "Well, this is Bert."

"Bert?" He quirked an eyebrow at her.

"I bought it from a mushroom grower named Bert who'd upgraded to a newer model. Every time anything went wrong, I'd yell, 'Oh, Bert.' The name kind of stuck. Hop in."

As he yanked open the passenger side door, it shrieked, probably something to do with the dent in the door. They glanced at each other over the top of the truck and in unison said, "Oh, Bert."

She backed the truck out and drove the short distance to the Chance place. She bumped down the narrow country lane towards her cottage and the rows of fields nearby. The sun was low and lit the fields golden.

He pulled a brown paper bag from his pocket, as though he'd forgotten it was there until he sat down. Placed it beside him on the seat.

"Did you buy something?" She wondered how he'd found time to shop being as busy as he was.

He shook his head. Opened the bag so it made a crinkling sound. "It was a gift. From the soap lady." He shook out the bag and a bar of bright yellow soap fell out, with a hand-written tag attached with twine. The loopy scroll read Kitchen Soap. "That was nice of her."

"I'm guessing there's a card on there with her phone number, in case you ever need more...soap."

It was a bitchy thing to say and she was immediately ashamed, but she'd had such a good view of the line-up of women who looked at Alexei – probably exactly the same way she looked at him.

He turned to her, and in the close proximity she could see the flecks of black in his eyes. "I don't ask for this, you know." He threw up his hands in a helpless gesture. "Women."

"This happens a lot?"

He grimaced. "All the time."

She almost laughed at his helpless expression and then realized she was as bad as the soap lady. As she geared down to avoid a rabbit leaping across the lane in front of her, she said. "Oh, God, I brought you tomatoes."

"No! That was different. I wanted your tomatoes. I mean, we're friends."

"Right. Exactly. Friends."

They pulled up to the shed where she parked the truck. They got out and she was once more conscious of the stiff hinge that shrieked out on his side of the car. The dim shed contained stacks of wooden crates and without even asking, he opened the back of the pick up and hefted out the crates she'd used today, stacking them with the others. "Okay, show me your operation."

"It's really not much. I don't want you getting all excited about nothing."

"Hey, I've already tasted some of what you grow here. You have lots to be excited about."

She led him out. The afternoon was fading but the last of the sun lit the land in a golden autumn light. She walked him down the rutted lane to where the fields stretched out in neat rows. "Most of it's fallow now, but the dark green shapes you can see are kale, which will grow all winter. I've got three varieties. There's also cabbage and squash. More potatoes to harvest but we're winding down."

He nodded, gazing at the rows with interest. "You must have more time on your hands at this time of year. What do you do in the more quiet months?"

She couldn't tell him about her newest project, online dating. "I do a little winter gardening still. I catch up on my reading, plan out the crops for next year, get more sleep."

"Sounds nice."

She glanced at him curiously. "You don't think it sounds like I'm a really boring woman who should get a life?"

He glanced at her in surprise. "No. I can see that you have a life, and it's a life that suits you."

Because she was talking, and concentrating on Alexei, she didn't notice the loose rock at her feet. As she stepped on it, she stumbled. She wouldn't have fallen, but as she put her hands out to steady herself Alexei grabbed her hand. She felt a rush of warmth and a current of electricity that pretty much shocked her to her core. As she righted herself, feeling suddenly breathless, she tried to retrieve her hand from his strong, warm clasp. But he held onto it for a moment and stopped walking so she was compelled to stop walking too. He opened out her fingers and ran his palm over hers. It was possibly the sexiest thing anyone had ever done to her. Her hands were far from her best feature: they were rough, working hands and she was embarrassed at how unfeminine they were. Alexi said, as though he had read her mind, "Your palms are calloused. I thought they would be." But he didn't say it in the tone of, "Girl, go get yourself a manicure." He said it more in a wondering tone, as though he actually liked her leathery working hands.

There was a moment, when he looked at her and she returned his gaze and felt trapped in a fantasy of her own creating. If she were a very foolish woman, she could believe that he was looking at her the way a man looks at a woman he wants to kiss. Her lips started to tingle and she could feel the longing build within her. There was nothing in all the world she wanted at this moment more than for him to lean forward and close the gap between them and put his mouth on hers. In her imagination, that's exactly what he did, but in reality, she burst into a flustered giggle and tugged her hand back. "You must be crazy. I have the hands of a longshoreman." She rubbed them together. "I've tried every hand cream, but it's no use."

"I like them," he said. And then he continued walking on. She fell into step beside him trying to pretend that she wouldn't relive that curious moment about seven thousand times in the next twenty-four hours. Just the fact that such a small gesture could curl her toes was more evidence that she really needed an actual man in her life and not this Greek god of a fantasy.

"Winter is a slow time for us, too. We still run the trucks, obviously, but for shorter hours. I usually only operate the one main truck and have a couple of backups for busy weekends. I guess we'll both have more time on our hands." He gazed over the fields. It was a glorious afternoon, she could see the green fields and in the distance the main house where she'd grown up. In the farther distance the hills looked like paper cutouts of dark green.

"What will you do with your extra time?" She asked, pretty much echoing what he'd asked her.

"I'm thinking about writing a cookbook," he said.

"A cookbook? Really?"

"Do you think it's a stupid idea?" He turned to her and she could see that her opinion actually mattered to him.

"No. I think it's a great idea. You're getting a real reputation in Portland." She'd never admit it, but she'd done an Internet search on him and discovered a few blogs and some online articles about his food truck. The only negative reviews he ever received were when people had waited in long lines in order to be fed. And even the complainers still raved about the food. "But do you really want to give away your secret recipes?"

"The thing about my recipes is, there's no real

secret. Anyone can make them. But, even with a recipe book, most people won't. It's a lot easier, let's face it, to run down to a food truck and order a ready-made meal than it is to source ingredients and take the time to actually prepare and cook the stuff. But, one of the reasons I want to do it is to talk about the core of good food. Starting with the best ingredients. And the value of good produce sourced locally. I was wondering if you might want to collaborate?"

She was so stunned she stopped walking and turned to stare at him. "You want me to collaborate on a cookbook?"

"Yeah. I was thinking about it."

"I burn toast. Cooking and I are not compatible."

He chuckled. "That's okay. Cooking is my gift. But your gift is to bring the most incredible food from the ground. And I have your emails so I know that you can write passionately on the subject. I think if we combined recipes with sections on growing food and the value of locally sourced food, complete with amazing pictures, we could really be on to something."

"Well, I don't know. I'd have to think about it." Of course, she wanted to jump at the chance to work with Alexei and to exchange more emails. He may have thought she was passionate about food, but she had a sneaking suspicion the passion coming out in her emails was deflected. When she raved about the color and richness and mineral content of an heirloom tomato what she was really saying was, "Alexei, I'm crazy about you. I want to spend every waking moment with you and have your babies." But, since she couldn't say those things, she rhapsodized about the lutein content of a homegrown tomato, and the benefits to the soil of growing complementary crops, when what she really wanted to say was, I want to grow beside you.

She became more enthusiastic about the idea as she mulled it over. "We could talk about natural pest control for the home gardener, which is mostly about having a strong plant that can ward off the bad guys but it's also about complementary planting. Plants that help each other out."

He nodded. "It's kind of like people. In a good relationship, each person brings different strengths. Together, they're stronger than either of them would be alone."

She was amazed to hear him say this and turned, her face lighting up. "Yes! That's exactly it. I use that analogy all the time. I know it's a romantic view of vegetables, but it works."

The shadows were beginning to lengthen, which made Alexei even more beautiful. His eyes became darker, the planes of his cheeks more pronounced, the full, sculpted lips only more desirable.

They shared another of those indescribable moments, of complete stillness and connection. She felt the pull to be with him, stronger than ever. If she didn't stop mooning over a man she could never have she was going to be in serious trouble.

But the man she could never have did not help. He

looked at her as though she were actually in his league, as though he found her attractive. Her with her unmanageable hair and hands as rough as a common labourer's.

"So," he said, "about the book, would you be interested?"

Would she be interested? In anything that allowed her to spend more time with the most beautiful man on the planet? And yet, a tiny voice of self-preservation suggested to her that this was probably a very, very bad idea. She'd been burned once when she flew too close to the sun and it hadn't ended well for her. She wasn't certain she could survive another plunge.

And yet...

It wasn't only the idea of spending time with him that appealed to her, but also the chance to express her views about food and healthy growing and healthy eating. Alexei had a big following, she knew that any book he authored would sell plenty of copies, and he was offering to give her a voice, to be part of something hip and fun and trendy. What a great way to slip in some more serious messages. So, she said, "Yes. I think I'm interested."

He seemed genuinely pleased by her answer. His easy grin gleamed in the deepening dusk. "That's great. I'll get back to you when I have details."

"Great." She glanced around, but it was really too late to show him much more. Only now did it occur to her that she needed to take him back to his truck but dinner at her parents was in an hour so it would actually be easier for him to stay here while she cleaned up. She had to take him into her house or look really peculiar. She really wished she'd thought things through better. She said, "I can drive you back to your truck now, or if you want to come to my place while I get ready, we can head over to my parents' place from here."

"Sure. That makes sense. I'll let Matt know he can drive the truck to your folks' place. He's been dying to drive that truck all day."

EIGHT

ALEXEI FOLLOWED THE sexiest woman who'd ever worn a pair of jeans into a cottage that looked like something out of a fairy tale. It was furnished more for comfort than style but he liked the overstuffed chintz couches, and the solid old wood pieces that someone, presumably Marguerite herself, had cleaned up. He very much liked the feeling that she was a person who walked the walk. Her personal values were everywhere from the composting bin in the kitchen, to furniture that was clearly recycled. A bookcase held books on yoga, gardening, meditation, herbal remedies and a handful of novels. A black and white cat glared at them from the depths of the couch, green eyes narrowed into slits. "What's the cat's name?"

"Ophelia."

"Ophelia?" He had a feeling there was a story here. "Like in Shakespeare?"

"Exactly like that. She was just a kitten when I found her half drowned in the river."

"I'm guessing she wasn't attempting suicide?" he

said, sitting on the couch beside the cat.

"My guess is that someone didn't want a kitten anymore."

"Why not just take her to a shelter?"

"Exactly."

He put his hand slowly towards the cat and Marguerite warned him, "She's not always the friendliest."

He didn't stop what he was doing, and as his knuckles gently touched the top of the cat's head, Ophelia leaned towards him. "Cats like me."

"Of course she does, she's female."

He imagined Marguerite had intended to mumble that under her breath so he pretended he didn't hear her. Instead, he kept his attention on petting and soothing Ophelia, who was completely open about her affection, purring and bumping at his fist. Unlike her human who was not big on showing her emotion.

Sometimes when their gazes met he felt a connection as deep and rich as anything he'd ever imagined, but she always backed away when things got interesting. Was it because of that blond guy he'd seen her kissing? He didn't seem her type. But then, how did he know what her type was?

And where had the crazy idea come from to co-author the book with her? He'd been approached by a local publisher about writing a cookbook and he'd been thinking about the project, but not very seriously. And then suddenly when he'd held her calloused hand in his and felt that incredible connection between them he'd grasped at straws. He felt that if he could entice her more deeply into his life, spend more time with her, that she'd maybe return his feelings. But then, as he began to describe the project off the top of his head, he realized that it was actually a good idea.

Who really needed another Greek cookbook? But a cookbook that combined some of the old recipes that his mother had brought with her from the homeland, as well as his own innovations, and tied them into a more local way of cooking and eating, seemed like it took the project to more interesting places.

Simply having a food truck guy author a cookbook was kind of hip and innovative, adding a local produce grower seemed like it added a layer of quirkiness he liked. Of course, he was going to have to convince the publisher that it was a great idea, but he had a feeling that he could make it work.

While he was making nice with Ophelia, Marguerite bustled around in the small kitchen. She said, "Would you like a cold beer?"

"It's like you read my mind?"

He heard the fridge open. She brought in two bottles. Local craft brews.

He clicked his bottle neck against hers and then drank. After working all day in the hot food truck, the beer went down well.

She sipped her own and stretched out her feet in front of her. "That was nice that you came. I think the food trucks added a big draw. I bet we doubled the money we brought in last year."

"Glad I could be part of it," he said. She leaned her head back against the couch and he wrapped his hand around the cold bottle, fighting the urge to push his fingers into her curls and pull her against him.

She turned her head and for a second he thought she'd read his mind. She leaned forward the tiniest bit and her lips softened. They were wet from the beer. She blinked and said, "Mind if I have a quick shower and get cleaned up?"

He gripped the cool glass tighter. "No. Not at all."

"You can shower after me, if you want."

"That would be great." He had been working all day, behind a hot stove serving many more customers than he had imagined would turn up at a country fair, and he felt like a shower would improve his general level of cleanliness immensely. He always kept a clean shirt in the food truck, so he'd at least be presentable for dinner.

Marguerite nodded and then headed down the hallway to where, presumably, both her bedroom and bathroom were located. In a few moments he heard the unmistakable sound of a shower running. He had a momentary, visceral image of a female form gauzy with steam. He blinked and pulled out his smartphone, forcing himself to concentrate on his emails, most of which seemed incredibly boring. There was one, however, from the publisher who was interested in the cookbook. He decided to throw out his strange new idea and see what happened, so he spent a few moments briefly laying out his idea before emailing back.

He was checking the day's news on an app when Marguerite said from behind him, "Bathroom's all yours."

He rose from the couch, eliciting a burp of annoyance from the cat snuggled beside him, and turned. Marguerite wore a long bathrobe. It was cream colored with big roses all over it. Her hair lay in long wet ringlets, her face was delicately flushed from the shower and her feet were bare. Lust curled in his belly, he couldn't stop it.

As though she had felt his inappropriate response, or hopefully, shared it, she took a nervous step back and said, "Let me show you the bathroom." She padded back down the hall and obediently he followed her.

The bathroom was the most elaborate in the house. As though after a day scrabbling around in the dirt she liked to wallow in the bathtub at the end of the day. It was a gorgeous, oversized tub, surrounded by lotions and creams and various potions all proclaiming to be organic, fair trade, and no doubt blessed by the Dalai Lama. A stack of towels rolled inside a basket looked as fluffy as clouds.

The space felt small, and intimate, and he saw a different side of Marguerite here, the sensuous feminine. There she stood, not two feet away from him, naked under her bathrobe, her face delicately flushed and those wet ringlets teasing him to touch her. He imagined that first, tentative kiss, rapidly deepening and then gave his head a shake. The woman had invited him into her home, trusted him to treat both it and her with respect, and here he was thinking of all the ways he could push her boundaries.

He nodded. "Thanks. I think I've got everything I need."

She stepped away out of the doorway. "I'll leave you to it then. There's a fresh toothbrush beside the sink."

And she was gone. Leaving nothing behind but the flowery, feminine scents swirling around him along with his hot thoughts.

He showered and dried himself off with a towel that a high-end spa would be proud to own and brushed his teeth with the purple toothbrush she'd left him, then wished only for a razor. He got dressed and left the bathroom, finding her in the living room. Her hair was still faintly damp as though she'd grown impatient drying it, and she'd slicked her lips with something glossy so they drew his attention. She wore a soft pair of jeans and a top in blues and greens that fitted loosely so it hinted at her curves. He thought she was the most beautiful thing he'd ever seen.

He noticed that she wasn't doing anything. Simply sitting there. When she'd left him alone, he'd immediately grabbed his phone and checked email. But she sat as though being quiet and still was enough. She didn't even have music playing. The tension and fatigue of a busy day slipped from his shoulders. "You are a very relaxing person."

Her lips tilted in a half smile. "When people say that to me I always wonder if it's a synonym for boring."

He wondered if the guy kissing her today told her she was a relaxing person. Which immediately made him feel less relaxed. "It isn't," he assured her.

"Good." The main house was only on the other side of her fields so they walked. The Chance home was a rambling structure that looked like what it was: a small cottage that had been added onto over many years, without the benefit of an architect, but it had a quirky charm very much like the Chance family itself.

He could see his food truck parked out front and said, "Do you mind if we detour so I can grab a clean shirt?"

"Of course."

"Just give me a second." The truck was unlocked, so he jumped up inside and grabbed his bag. "I've got plenty of salad left. Should I take it in for the dinner?"

"Yes, Daphne would love it."

She stepped up into the truck just as he yanked off his T-shirt. He caught her staring at his naked chest and, for the first time, she didn't look away.

Maybe she'd confused him a lot of the time, but at this moment he'd bet his truck that she was as drawn to him as he was to her.

Maybe it was a crazy bet, but he hadn't become successful without taking crazy chances before.

Hope bloomed, along with something much hotter as she continued to stare.

NINE

MARGUERITE HAD NOT realized that Alexei was about to strip off his shirt. He gave no warning, no hint that would give her time to shield her gaze—or run away.

Did he have to be so beautiful without his shirt on? Could he not have sported at least one small roll of fat or a really bad tattoo? Instead, his torso was as spectacular as the rest of him.

She knew he'd caught her staring, and she couldn't seem to drag her gaze away. Everything about him was too perfect. Way. Too. Perfect. Her palms itched to touch the dusky skin, to trace the arrow of hair that led over that taut belly and disappeared behind the button of his jeans. The space inside the truck seemed suddenly so small she felt she'd suffocate in her own lust.

Here he'd invited her in with nothing in mind but salad, and she was thinking how she wanted to plant her lips on the warm skin of his belly, let her hands trail... What was she doing?

She blinked. "Salad!"

His eyes crinkled in amusement. "Right. Salad."

While he swiftly donned a creamy cotton shirt, every part of her wanted to cry "No!" as he covered up, and she had to hold herself back from yanking the shirt off again, she turned her focus to vegetables. Cold, refrigerated, extremely unsexy vegetables.

He came up to her side, taking down a large stainless steel bowl, and dumping the already prepared Greek salad from the white industrial container. "It's not exactly a crystal serving dish, but it's all I have."

"Honestly, she'll be thrilled. My mom's dinners aren't exactly fancy. We go more for comfort food, and plenty of it, than anything high-end or gourmet."

"Then my salad will fit right in." While he was talking, he sprinkled oregano over the top of the salad and then shook a bottle of his premade salad dressing and squirted it over the luscious looking salad. Then he gave it a quick and very professional toss. She watched the crumbles of white feta, the dark shiny olives, the rich red tomatoes, the chunks of dark green pepper and cucumber and the slivers of red onion tumble and meld in the dressing.

It was a Greek salad like any other, but somehow, whatever he did with the dressing and the quality of the ingredients made this salad stand out. Also, she had to take some credit for the fact that he was now using more produce grown in Washington and Oregon. As she stood watching, he reached into the bowl, picked up a particularly ripe-looking tomato and popped it into her mouth. She nodded enthusiastically as the flavors danced on her tongue, the rich, sweet burst of tomato complimented with a dressing that expertly enhanced the flavors. "It's perfect."

He was looking at her intently. He said, "You may not cook, but you sure enjoy food. I want to cook for you."

She was so surprised she nearly choked on her tomato. "You cooked for me today. You brought me over that beautiful souvlaki."

He shook his head impatiently. "No. I mean really cook for you. I took serious chef training you know."

"I'm a vegetarian. I always feel like I'm letting a chef down when I go for dinner."

He shook his head. "Any good chef should be able to make a vegetarian meal that's outstanding." Then he grinned down at her. "Now you've challenged my talent. You'll have to let me cook for you and prove I can impress you."

She had no idea what he was offering her. Was he talking about cooking for her at his house? Here in the truck? Throwing something on the barbecue at her place? She wasn't sure how to answer him. The silence lengthened. He said, "It would be a casual thing. You can come to my place, I'll cook you a nice veggie meal and we can think about our cookbook."

Okay, so it was more of a business deal. At his place. Where he lived, and slept, and all his things were around him. She said, "I'd like that." As they headed out of the truck, she was so surprised and confused by what was going on between her and

117

Alexei that she nearly missed what was going on between his brother and her sister standing in the shadows. They almost stumbled onto an intensely passionate embrace.

She always thought of her sister, Rose, as a cool, professional woman who was always in control. But the woman twined around Matt did not look cool or in control. She was lip locked with Alexei's brother so tightly it looked like it would take the jaws of life to get them apart.

Alexei came up behind her and, unlike her, didn't stand there frozen in horror. Instead he called out, "Hey you two, get a room!" For a second nothing happened. It seemed as though Rose and Matt hadn't even heard him. And then, slowly, Matt pulled back as though it hurt him to do so. He said, "Your timing always did suck, little bro."

But he didn't look irritated, even in the dim light she could see that his eyes were sparkling and he looked as happy as she'd ever seen him.

And Rose! Rose was practically glowing. To Marguerite's shock she lifted her hands and wiped tears from her eyes. Marguerite could count on the fingers of one hand the times she had seen Rose cry, and have plenty of fingers left. Then she saw that there was something very large and diamond-like sparkling from the ring finger of her left hand.

She ran forward. "Oh my gosh, are you…?"

Rose held up her hand and then clasped Marguerite to her in a tight hug. "Engaged?" She said in a shaky voice. "Yes." Beside her she heard the noisy embrace of the two brothers with much backslapping involved.

Then they switched partners and she found herself being pulled into Matt's embrace while Alexei hugged Rose. After a moment when they'd both said congratulations, Alexei pulled Rose's hand into his and she could see the extent of the Tiffany ring.

Alexei turned to his brother and shook his head, "Dude, that is so Greek. What happened, they didn't have any bigger ones?"

However, Marguerite knew her sister. Rose had extremely high-end tastes, and she didn't think having an oversized diamond was going to be a real problem for her.

Alexei wasn't done teasing. "Did you spend all your money on the diamond, so you couldn't take the woman out for dinner and propose to her properly? You had to go on bended knee in your future in-laws' gravel parking area?"

Matt threw up his hands in a very Mediterranean fashion. He said, "I had plans. I was going to take her somewhere really romantic and propose in style. You know, somewhere we'd tell our grandchildren about and it would make a great story. But I had the ring burning a hole in my pocket and we got here, and we started kissing and suddenly the ring was out of my pocket and on her finger. I don't really know how it happened."

"I think it's romantic," Marguerite insisted. "This

is our home, where Rose grew up. And, you know, if you tried to orchestrate something romantic, Rose would've known what was going on. But I'll tell you one thing, I know my sister, and you just surprised the hell out of her."

"She's right," Rose said, her voice sounding a little shaky. "You did surprise the hell out of me." Then she laughed. "But in a good way." She and Matt gazed at each other and there was no doubt that, however he proposed, their being together was meant to be.

"When are you getting married?"

"I haven't got that far," Matt said. "I wasn't sure she'd say yes."

Alexei said, "You know, our mother is going to have something to say about that. *My Big Fat Greek Wedding*'s going to have nothing on Mrs. Vasilopoulos."

"And our Mom is going to be so happy," Marguerite said, already anticipating the cries of joy and the dancing around the room that this engagement would cause.

Matt puffed up with pride. He said, "Well, let's go do it. I should probably ask your father for his permission."

Rose snorted. "Please. We're not living in a Jane Austen novel. Besides, you saved Jack Chance's life, I think he is going to give you his daughter. Not a problem."

"That's kinda what I was hoping."

The four of them headed towards the house and

suddenly Rose stopped. She said, "You know, I don't think this is the right moment to tell the family."

They all stopped walking and Matt asked, "Why not?"

In the gathering gloom Rose glanced at Marguerite. "This is our mom's big day. She was the Queen of the Fall Fair. Let's tell them next time we're down here when things are more normal."

"That'll be a long wait," Matt said and they all laughed.

Marguerite liked the thoughtfulness that her sister was showing.

"You know she'll be happy for you," she said softly.

Rose gazed at the beautiful diamond on her finger for a long moment and then she put it to her mouth and kissed the stone before slowly withdrawing it and handing it back to Matt. "Can you put that back in its box and keep it for me?"

He sent her a wry grin. "This is your way of making me take you out for dinner and make a fool of myself in front of all the other dinner guests, isn't it?"

She laughed. "No. Really. I only want to get engaged once. I think the way you did it was perfect. I have never been so surprised in all my life. Let's just keep the news to the four of us for now."

Matt took out an iconic blue box from his pocket and carefully received the ring from his brand-new fiancée. He said, "Can you believe it? Henpecked already."

"Get used to it bro," Alexei said. But he winked at Marguerite as he said the words.

Maybe no one else knew about the engagement, but dinner that night was as happy as any family occasion she could remember. It was great to have Paisley back in their midst. In fact, more than half her sibs were there.

When they arrived, Daphne was thrilled with the Greek salad. "I was in the kitchen thinking I didn't have enough greens and here you are with this lovely salad."

"Beware of Greeks bearing gifts, Daphne," Matt said, then presented her with a box of the handmade chocolate truffles from the fair.

"Oh, you boys are too cute!"

Marguerite had no idea how her mother did it, but after a crazy day of running the fall fair she was somehow able to pull together a dinner for almost twenty people. She could smell her mom's meatloaf cooking in the kitchen. Well, she knew exactly how Daphne did it. She had a freezer full of dishes that she pre-prepared. They weren't gourmet fare, but good, substantial dishes that she could pull out, thaw, and thunk onto the old wooden table that had served as the Chance family gathering spot for decades. And, if pressed, she could do it in about sixty minutes.

"Are you freakin kidding me?" Cooper yelled from the direction of the bathroom. "Everybody, get in here. You've got to see this!"

"Oh, no," Iris cried, "Did that squirrel make a nest

in the towels again?"

They all pounded down to the bathroom at the end of the hall and when Marguerite was able to push her way in, she saw what they were all laughing at. "It's not a squirrel," Alexei said behind her. "It's a poodle."

"A very pink poodle," she agreed. Sitting on the back of the toilet was a bright pink knitted poodle with black button eyes. "It's a toilet roll cover," Daphne said from behind them. As though that wasn't obvious. "Prescott bought it for me."

"Prescott? The famous architect known for his minimalism?" James asked very loudly.

Everyone turned. Prescott, who usually appeared so devoid of emotion that Evan had once told the rest of the kids he was half Vulcan, looked at the floor. "I had to buy something. It was the only way I could get away from Edna May Tittlebury."

"It was very thoughtful of you, Scott," Daphne said, rubbing his shoulder before heading back toward the kitchen.

"And it is so getting regifted to you at Christmas, son," Jack informed him.

"Welcome to my family," Marguerite said as Cooper firmly shut the bathroom door on the crowd of them.

He'd met most of them throughout the day, but she refreshed him on all the names.

As they headed back down the hall, Jack said, "I wish you'd park that truck in Hidden Falls every day. The food was fantastic. Only next time, don't bring my heart doctor down with you in the truck, so I can go back for seconds."

"I'll go help your mom in the kitchen, Alex said to her, touching her arm as he went by, exactly as though they were a couple.

She was setting the table when Paisley yelled from the living room. "Hey Mom, you're going to be on TV. The Hidden Falls fair is up next."

Once more feet pounded, this time into the living room where everyone gathered around the big screen TV that Jack had finally been allowed to buy after he'd been bedridden with a heart ailment.

Jack and Daphne flopped on the big couch with Paisley and Cooper. Rose and Matt shared a big armchair, Holly and Prescott another, and everyone else sat on the floor. Alex settled beside Marguerite and Lucy, the family's golden retriever, walked among them, sensing the excitement, her wagging until she flopped beside Marguerite and put her head on her knee.

"That's a great TV, Jack," Alex said, as a toothpaste commercial played.

"Thanks. I damn near had to croak before Daphne would let me have a decent size TV."

"Shhh," said his loving wife as her face came up on the screen. The announcer said, "It's Autumn Festival time and we're here in Hidden Falls, Oregon where the annual Fall Harvest Fair took place today. With me is Daphne Chance, this year's fair coordinator. Daphne, take us around and show us some of the attractions."

"I'd be happy to," Daphne said. "Of course, our fair isn't only for fun. We raise money to keep after school programs funded for at risk children." She turned to the camera and announced, "Because every community has an obligation to look after its kids."

"Right on, Daphne," Jack said.

Then the camera cut to the Hidden Falls Fiddlers, panned around the stalls. A couple of cute little kids, one holding cotton candy and the other an ice cream cone, said it was, "Really fun."

"What's on that kid's face?" Cooper asked, squinting. "Did someone pelt him with a tomato?"

"It's a fire-breathing dragon," Paisley said.

"Shhh," Daphne said.

On screen, Daphne walked the reporter right up to Alexei's Greek. "And this year we were lucky enough to get support from five food trucks. This is Alexei Vasilopoulos and his brother Matt. They're not only gorgeous, but they make fantastic Greek food." In the background, Alex and Matt were so busy serving customers, they probably never even noticed they were being filmed.

"Mo-th-er!" Iris groaned.

"What? That's excellent free publicity I gave you, right Alex?"

"Absolutely," he said, grinning.

"But you were hitting on two young guys right on TV."

"Oh, of course I wasn't."

"Dad?"

Jack thought for a moment and said, "I want the big screen TV in the divorce."

Alex leaned closer and whispered, "I am crazy about your family."

With Alexei as Daphne's sous chef, dinner was a lot more fancy than usual. One minute he was taking his big bowl of glorious, fresh Greek salad into the kitchen, and the next thing she knew, things began to emerge from the kitchen that she only half recognized.

There was her mother's meatloaf, but with a sauce that took it from the pedestrian to the sublime. He whipped up garlic and herb butters to serve with the long baguettes that Iris had brought from the bakery.

He'd added some extra spices and some sort of crunchy topping to the massive dish of chicken casserole. Along with her mother's vegetarian lasagna, he'd whipped up a quinoa dish with kale and beans and flavorings she didn't recognize but were delicious.

Luckily, since Jack's heart troubles, he'd been dissuaded from turning out his homemade wine that tasted like drain cleaner and packed a punch stronger than moonshine. Evan and Prescott had made a wine run earlier so the wine was excellent. There was also beer and ice tea.

She'd half hoped that Iris and Geoff would tell everyone about the baby, but the dinner dragged on and there was no announcement.

Alexei sat beside her at dinner and she had to fight all her instincts not to feel thrilled to have him there, as though he were making a point, when likely he'd sat himself there because she was the only person he really knew at the dinner apart from Matt, and obviously he wasn't going to sit beside his older brother. She knew enough about boys to understand that.

He felt so good sitting there beside her, gorgeous, solid and strong. Everyone loved him. Her mother, her father, all her sibs, even his own brother obviously thought enough of him to take time out of a successful career as a surgeon to help out in the food truck.

That was the trouble with Alexei. It wasn't only that he was gorgeous; lots of guys were gorgeous and left her cold. He was also nice. The kind of man who donated a Saturday, and a lot of profit, to help out kids in a town he didn't even live in. Everyone loved him, she reminded herself, which made it doubly scary for her to even think of him as a romantic interest.

Marguerite liked to think of herself as the kind of flower that perhaps blooms in a woodland meadow. Easily overlooked and very easily eclipsed by the fancier show off blooms. And she was fine with that. But for her to think of herself with Alexei was like putting a shrinking violet in the shadow of a huge sunflower. Sunflowers needed other sunflowers or big, bold blooms that could stand up. A violet would be totally eclipsed. It wasn't that she minded most of the time. She accepted her limitations. And yet, for some reason, this woodland violet had a yearning that was growing stronger by the day for the biggest, brightest, sunflower she'd ever seen.

After dinner, the family gathered in its usual noisy collection all over the living room. In a tribe where if you wanted attention you generally had to talk louder than anyone else, she was pleased to see that Alexei and Matt could hold their own. She imagined that in a Greek family the same rules applied as in the Chance family.

Matt was staying overnight. He and Rose had already commandeered the guest cottage on the property. That meant Alexei was driving back by himself. By the time he was ready to leave, he had charmed all of her family but nobody could possibly feel a yearning as potent as hers.

When he was ready to leave, Daphne insisted on hugging him and thanking him profusely for taking part in the fall fair. "It added so much pizzazz to our little event to have food trucks this year. Thank you so much for putting the word out and for taking part. I hope you'll do it again next year."

"Love to. I had a great time today." He turned to say good-bye to everyone and then Daphne said, "Marguerite, why don't you walk Alexei out?"

Before she could answer, Alexei said, "I'd really like that."

With every fiber of her being she forced herself not to blush. She was fairly certain that every fiber of her being let her down as she felt heat crawl up into her cheeks. "Sure," she mumbled and, keeping her head down, followed him out of that overheated, overcrowded house and into the relative cool of the evening.

She glanced up and caught him gazing at her with amusement. She said, "I'm sorry. I think her success at running the fair has gone to Mom's head. Now she's moved on to matchmaking."

He chuckled softly and she was immediately glad that she had been honest with him about her mother's very unsubtle antics. "It's a mother thing," he said. "Believe me, my mother is worse than yours. She's so desperate for grandchildren she pretty much grills every woman we meet on whether she wants kids or not."

She glanced up at him with concern. It was one thing to feel embarrassed for herself, but her sister Rose had just become engaged to his brother. "You know Rose doesn't want kids, right?"

He nodded. "Which puts me in the firing line for producing grandchildren."

She wanted to tell him that she loved children and would be more than happy to throw herself on that production line, starting right this second, to make his mother a grandmother.

"And do you? Um, want kids?"

"Sure. I love kids." The evening air felt soft. A light breeze ruffled the leaves in the trees. He said, "How about you?"

He was only making conversation, she reminded

herself, as she replied, "I do."

"I had a good time tonight. It was good to see your family all together."

"Not all together. For that you'd probably want to have a couple of stiff drinks first."

"My family is Greek. You got nothing on us."

She merely smiled, but thought how very much she'd like to see him with all of his family.

They arrived at his truck, then stood awkwardly for a moment. He said, "Well, I'd better get going. I'll call you about the cookbook."

In that moment he leaned swiftly forward and touched his lips to hers, so fast she barely had time to register that Adonis himself was kissing her when he'd pulled away and was opening the door to his food truck.

"I'll call you," he said.

She couldn't find the words to reply and simply stood there, with her lips tingling, speechless.

TEN

"WHAT DO YOU mean, he kissed you?" Rose squealed. Rose was not the sort of woman who squealed or became all girly over a simple kiss, which pretty much confirmed Marguerite's opinion that the natural order of things had been turned upside down.

Marguerite, Rose and Iris were neck deep in thermal hot spring water, supposedly soaking their cares away. Rose had decreed that the Chance women would have a spa day today, but Paisley had to study, Daphne had left early to look after the post-fair administration. Evan and Caitlyn and Holly and Prescott had left after a late brunch.

There were three levels to the hot pool: warm, hot, and hottest. Iris was always the one who wanted to go into the hottest of the pools but not today. She insisted they stay in the warm pool. Marguerite knew why, of course, but so far, Iris hadn't told Rose her news. Which was why Marguerite, feeling the atmosphere grow awkward between the three of them, had suddenly blurted out the incident that was obsessing her at the moment. That kiss had been so swift that all she could remember was the fleeting heat and press of his lips against hers. If she could time travel, she'd go back to that moment to live in it for an hour, or maybe a few days.

"He likes you. Anyone can see he likes you," Iris joined in, sounding a lot less shocked than Rose.

"Well, of course he likes her, but, you know, kissing?" Then Rose shifted in the water and focused on Marguerite. "Did you like it? I wasn't sure if you felt that way about Alexei. I thought maybe you were seeing someone?"

She wondered if her sister had wormed out of Iris that she was Internet dating, or whether the 60 Minutes act was Rose's way of caring. She said, "Alexei's great. And I'm not really seeing anyone. I've had a couple of dates recently, but nothing serious."

Rose continued, "So, do you like Alex?"

The pool seemed to rise a few degrees in temperature. "Of course, I like him. Everyone likes him."

"You know what I mean, do you like him, like him. Did you like kissing him?"

"You know Iris's double chocolate fudge brownies?"

Rose nodded.

"Kissing him was better."

"Oh, come on. He is human." Rose glanced from one to the other. "Isn't he?"

Iris contemplated the question as though it were

serious. "A man that good looking? Kisses like an angel. And he cooks? I don't know."

"Oh, stop it," Marguerite said, trying not to laugh. "It was only the world's fastest kiss. I don't even know why I told you."

Iris nudged her. "Because kissing's where everything starts."

Rose said, "If we're going to talk about sex, I need to move to a hotter pool." She began to pull herself up, revealing the top part of a sculpted body that she and her personal trainer worked at diligently.

Iris stopped her with a hand on Rose's shoulder. "Wait. I need to talk to you."

Rose sank slowly back down into the water and drilled Iris with a look that was partly medical and partly big sister. "Aha," she said. "I wondered."

Marguerite considered the irony that one sister was pregnant, the other engaged, and the only one who had so far spilled their news was her telling them about the world's most innocuous kiss.

There was something about the rhythm of sisters. Even though they didn't see each other all that often, when the three of them got together they fell back into patterns. She smiled to herself, knowing that they probably always would.

Iris raised her hands in the air causing water droplets to stream down her arms and plop onto the surface of the pool. "Okay. I'm pregnant!"

In her line of work, Rose dealt with pregnant women all the time, but this was her sister and the first pregnancy in the Chance family. Even though she had to have known what the news was, she still squealed and jumped up to give her blushing sister a noisy and very wet hug. "I'm so happy for you. Really, really happy for you."

Iris waved her hands in front of her face. "You're going to make me cry. But then everything from seeing a baby in a carriage to kittens on a TV commercial makes me cry these days."

"Hormones," Rose stated. "Lots and lots of hormones." Then she immediately switched into Doctor mode. "Are you taking pregnancy vitamins?"

"Yes. I started them months ago in fact."

"Good. And how are you feeling generally?"

"Scared, that's how I feel. Scared. I have wanted this for so long, wanted it so badly, that on some level I can't believe it's true."

Rose placed a reassuring hand on her sister's shoulder. "That's not unusual. When you've wanted to get pregnant, it can be frightening when it actually comes true. I see it a lot in my practice. Have you had a scan yet?"

"In two weeks."

"How many weeks along are you?"

"About eight."

"Good. Do you want me to come with you to the scan?"

Rose was a busy, busy woman, and for her to offer was a very big deal. Iris waved a hand in front of her face once more. "No," she replied. "Geoff is coming with me. But thank you so much for offering."

"You call me the minute it's over and tell me everything. I can't take you on since we're sisters, but I can refer you to an excellent OB/GYN if you want me to."

Iris shook her head. "I've been going to Dr. Bailey forever. I trust her."

Rose nodded. "The offer stands if you want a second opinion or anything."

"Thanks. I'll let you know."

"Does Mom know?" she asked in a puzzled tone as all three of them knew that if their mother knew about the pregnancy she'd never have acted so relatively cool and normal last night.

Iris shook her head. "I'm not ready to tell her yet. It will all seem too real, and if anything happened..."

"You're young and healthy. Statistics are on your side. Plus, who would you want to support you if anything did go wrong but Mom?" Which was exactly what Marguerite had said.

"I know you're right. I can't explain it. I just have to work through this fear, I guess."

"Well, if you need to talk, you can always reach me. And congratulations again. This is happy news!"

Knowing that Iris was close to tears again, Marguerite said, "Does anyone else have any happy news to share?" And raised her eyebrows significantly in Rose's direction.

She threw her arms in the air, much the way Iris had done earlier, so water rivulets danced off her toned arms. "What can I say? He got to me. Matt and I are getting married!"

Iris's squeal was every bit as heartfelt as Rose's had been earlier. She jumped up so fast she caused waves to ripple around them as she threw her arms around her sister. "Oh my gosh! I can't believe it. Another sister getting married."

"This is quite a day. A first kiss, an engagement, and a baby. Ladies, I think we need to get the pregnant lady out of this hot water and go treat ourselves to some manicures and pedicures." She waved her ring hand in the air. "Personally, I've got a very large rock to show off. I wouldn't want my fingernails to let me down."

So the three of them donned the plush white robes provided by the spa and padded to the beauty treatment area. When Marguerite's aesthetician began her manicure, the woman frowned over her hands. "Are you a rock climber?"

"No."

The woman grabbed a pumice stone and started scrubbing. "I've only ever seen hands like this on a rock climber before."

She resisted the urge to sit on her hands, since she was here in order to have them improved. She sighed, unable to repress the memory of Alexei running his palm over her much rougher one. She said, "I grow vegetables for a living." Thinking rock climbing sounded a lot more glamorous.

The aesthetician shook her head sadly. "Honey, you need to think about gardening gloves."

ELEVEN

SHE WOULD NOT feel nervous, she told herself, as she pulled her truck into an unfamiliar driveway in Portland's Hawthorne District. Alexei had invited her to his home in order to plan out their cookbook, talk about how his recipes would integrate with her short essays on organic gardening. The publisher had been quite enthusiastic about combining the two. According to Alexei, she was so enthusiastic she had begun talking about putting together some kind of a TV pilot.

She could understand anyone wanting to put Alexei on television. She could see him as a glamorous TV chef working from a food truck.

The project was beginning to seem real, especially as it included a budget for a photographer who would take some professional shots of Alexei cooking in the food truck and even photos of her small organic farm.

In another man, the promise to cook for her might sound like a real date, but she and Alexei were two people who worked with food for their professions and were planning to write a cookbook together. Of course he was going to cook for her, as she was going to grow vegetables for him. She got out of her truck and then hefted the small crate of kale and potatoes that she had brought with her. She'd hesitated over getting a bottle of wine but she didn't want him to think she had the wrong idea about tonight so she stuck with the vegetables.

He lived in a small bungalow that had to be nearly a century old. A small covered porch was set in front of a shiny black front door flanked by two pots. Where anyone else might have a small topiary in the pot, he had actual olive trees growing in terra-cotta pots that appeared dusty with age. She'd bet her entire crop of winter cabbage that the pots had come all the way from Greece. They were tucked up against the wall of the house to shelter them from the elements, but wondered if they'd survive a winter out here.

She rang the doorbell and waited. A moment later the door opened and, as she took step to enter, Alexei took a step toward her, nearly treading on her toe and bumping her body back. She glanced up in alarm to find a very strange expression on his face, something close to panic. "I'm really sorry," he said in an urgent whisper. "My mother's here."

She tried to ignore the flash of heat on all the parts of her that he'd touched. "Your mother's here? Does she live with you?"

"God no. My mother gets these *feelings*." He put air quotes around the word. "Then she jumps on a plane and comes out to bother my brother and me."

"Maybe she is psychic, I mean your brother just got engaged."

"She is not psychic. She's nosy. And interfering. She's in my kitchen right now taking over. I'm really sorry. I wanted to cook for you."

She was charmed. First, that he was so clearly flustered and unable to control his own mother. And that he wanted to warn her. She said, "I don't mind." And she didn't.

"Honest, if you want to turn tail and run, I won't blame you."

She shook her head. "I can handle Mama."

"You only say that because you haven't met her yet." He took the box from her with a muttered word of thanks and then led her inside. Where it smelled fantastic.

As she followed Alexei into his house, a small, round woman came bustling out of what was clearly the kitchen. She had a red and white striped apron wrapped around her waist. She had dark curly hair and a swarthy complexion. At first glance, it seemed that all Alexei had inherited from her was her large, expressive eyes. These took Marguerite in from top to toe with one sweeping, comprehensive glance.

"Mama, allow me to present my friend Marguerite Chance." Marguerite noticed that he put the emphasis on the word friend. "Marguerite this is Eleni Vasilopoulos. My mother."

Marguerite had to bend down to accept the embrace being offered her. Alexei's mother kissed her soundly on one cheek and then the other and then drew back scrutinizing her with no embarrassment whatsoever. She turned to Alexei. "But she is beautiful. You did not tell me this woman was so beautiful."

Before he could speak Marguerite jumped in. "No. Really, I'm not."

The woman shook her head. "North Americans don't understand beauty. She is beautiful in the Greek way of beauty. And, you know, the Greeks invented beauty. Also architecture, art, thought, sports and literature."

Alexi broke into something short and sharp in Greek. His mother answered just as sharply. Even without hearing the words she was pretty sure she could figure out what they were saying to each other.

Eleni Vasilopoulos said, "You are the sister of the doctor who is marrying my other son."

"Rose Chance. Yes, she is my sister."

The older woman nodded and narrowed her eyes. "You like children?"

She could feel Alexei getting ready to tell his mother off again in Greek so very quickly she said, "Yes. I love children." And simply to save herself getting the next question she said, "and I hope to have some myself one day."

Alexei took the box of produce and shoved it at his mother. The woman gazed down at the dark green of the kale and the lumpy shaped potatoes with a little dirt still clinging to them. She touched them as though they were a box of newly hatched baby chicks. She nodded. "This is how food should be." Then she shook her head. "I apologize for the food. He's my son, he should know how to cook for guests, but he has only one dessert. You come to my house and see what Greek hospitality is. Baklava, galaktoboureko, koulourakia and kourabiethes." She sighed.

"We'll be fine, Mama."

She glanced at Marguerite and then back at Alexei. She said something to him in Greek and turned away. As though she were repeating the same phrase but had forgotten to speak Greek she said in English, "I like this one. She could be Greek."

Alexei said, "You know what else is Greek? Tragedies about interfering mothers!"

"I have to go now. I wanted to serve the dinner and get a nice picture of you both with the food, but your brother needs me."

"That's really too bad, Mama. I'll get your coat."

The next time she saw Alexei's mother the woman had her coat on and had come to say goodbye. "I am having dinner with Matthew and Rose," she said. "To celebrate the engagement. But, of course, we will have a proper engagement party in our home to welcome your sister into our family." She touched Marguerite on the shoulder. "You must come. Alexei will bring you."

It didn't feel so much like an invitation as an order. But still, as they cheek kissed, she said, "Thank you. Enjoy your evening."

She then issued Alexei a spate of instructions that

ended with her calling him Beautiful Boy and giving him resounding kisses on either cheek. After she left, he turned to Marguerite and shook his head. "I am so sorry about that."

"Don't be." She struck a pose. "She likes this one."

He laughed, as she'd meant him to. And surprised her by saying, "My mother may be a pain in the ass but she has good taste in women."

Since she didn't know how to respond, she asked, "Can I have a tour of your house?"

"Sure. Absolutely." He gestured around the small living room. "As you can see, it's a work in progress." As she glanced around, she understood what he meant. He'd removed all the old brick from the fireplace but hadn't put in a new front yet. The sills of the charming old windows had been stripped and awaited new paint. But he clearly used the room. A few pieces of dark leather furniture dotted the room, and a flat screen hung above the wall where one day the new fireplace would be. Mentally, she replaced the furniture with something more contemporary and more comfortable, added some throw cushions and tried a few of her favorite colors on the beige walls. She liked the images her imagination was spitting out. "This room will be charming," she said.

As though he'd correctly read her unexpressed thoughts, he said, "I put all my extra time and money into the kitchen. Come, see."

He took her hand and led her out of the living

room and down the short hallway toward the tantalizing aroma of cooking food.

"Ah," she said, understanding immediately that he really had put all his resources into this room. The kitchen was sleek and efficient as well as being intimate somehow. She felt its utility, from the pots hanging from the pot rack above the six burner gas range, to the stone counter tops, and industrial fridge, but the kitchen was also warm and homey. Corner shelves held pieces of brightly painted Greek pottery. A small eating area contained a round table set for two. When she looked at it, he said, "The house has a dining room, if you prefer, but I thought we'd eat in here. I can show you what I'm doing while I cook and we can talk about the book."

"That's perfect." Behind the small table was a set of French doors that led out into a garden. As she headed toward them and pressed her nose against the glass he reached behind her and flipped a switch illuminating his backyard. "This must be so beautiful in the summer," she said.

She could see an enormous lavender bush so bounteous she could almost smell the fragrance from inside the kitchen. The dark spiky leaves of rosemary reached skyward and he even had a potted bay tree close to his backdoor, like the olive trees at the front, sheltered from the elements. She suspected that during a really bad winter he'd lose it, but from the size of the tree, this one had already been growing for a few years quite happily. Naturally, in her mind's eye, she turned half of the lawn area into vegetable beds to complement his herb garden. The rock wall would be a beautiful spot for some raspberry canes.

When she turned back into the room she found him looking at her in some amusement. "What?"

He said, "You were planning vegetable beds out there, weren't you?"

She couldn't help but laugh. "Busted. I can't help myself. I see arable land and I want to put beautiful fruit and vegetables on it."

"I bet you'll inspire all kinds of people to do the same thing." He moved to stir a delicious-smelling pot on the stove. "I really wanted to cook for you myself but I can't lie to you. My mother's been interfering since the moment she got here. It's not me who is going to be feeding you tonight, it's my mother."

"That's okay. I bet she taught you everything you know."

He sent her an enigmatic glance. "Not everything."

TWELVE

THE WONDERFUL THING about having dinner with Alexei was that he made the preparation and cooking of food an adventure. He would be great on a cooking show. Apart from the movie-star good looks, he could cook and explain at the same time. He didn't need to think about what he was going to say, nor did he have to stop what he was doing in order to speak. He crumpled a handful of fresh oregano in his palm, then opened it and wafted the fresh bruised herbs under her nose as he explained, "Sure, you can use dried herbs. But when you use fresh oregano, the way we do in Greece, you'll get a truer flavor."

He talked about the olives and the olive oil and the kind of soil that grew the best sorts of olives even as he glugged gold liquid into a pan. It was as though he were having a conversation, not only with her, but with the food itself. "It's like you talk to the dish you're cooking," she said finally.

"Absolutely. It's not only me talking to the food but ingredients communicating with each other. It's like with you growing the plants, some help each other and some don't. Certain foods don't like each other. They've had a feud going on for generations. Combine them and they will make your dinner taste all wrong. You know? Like it's in a big fight. But, you put foods together that already like each other, or introduce a couple of new ingredients and let them flirt with each other, and it's amazing what can happen. It's like magic."

She watched, fascinated, as he diced and stirred, sautéed and tasted, murmured over the pots like a magician and added a sprinkle of this, a splash of that. His hands worked rapidly, making knives and spoons dance and play like musical instruments. When he paused for a second, she noticed a scar on his index finger. It was a paler ripple of flesh and fascinated her as everything about him fascinated her.

She said, "What happened to you there?" She touched the puckered skin with her fingertip.

He peered at it. "I burned it," he said matter-of-factly.

"Don't you remember when? It looks like it was painful."

He shrugged. "Could've been the time I was working in a kitchen that caught fire. We had to put the flames out so we could finish cooking dinner. The restaurant was fully booked." He grinned in memory. "That was a crazy night. Or it might've been one time I lost my concentration around something hot when I shouldn't have." He opened both his hands out and offered them to her and she could see scars and burn marks. They enthralled her the way a map or piece of art might fascinate her. "What about this one?" She ran her fingertip across a scar that was like a white line drawn across the pad of his palm. She couldn't seem to stop her hands from touching his.

"Sharp knife, dull wits."

"Come on. I can see the stitch marks. You remember this one. It bought you a trip to the emergency room."

He chuckled. "I've had a few of those. I think that one was a knife sharpening accident."

"A knife sharpening accident?"

He grinned at her. "You have to admit I'm a good knife sharpener. It was a very sharp knife. Look how clean that slice is."

After she'd admired his scars and burns, he took one of her hands in his.

He opened the fingers slowly, one at a time. And he ran the tip of his fingertip across the callused bumps at the top of her palm. "How about you? How did you get those?"

She looked down at her palm as though it were a journal recounting the history of her life. "Pulling potatoes? Digging? Hoeing? Lifting heavy crates? Some or all of those things."

"How about these?" He touched the leathery spots on her fingers. She shivered when he touched her.

"I think that was the time I planted squash and forgot to wear gardening gloves."

"Do you ever wear garden gloves?"

She shook her head. "Almost never. I like the feel of the earth beneath my fingers. There's something magical about breaking apart a lump of clay and feeling its texture, and the moisture within the soil. I want to touch the earth and the plants I work with. With gloves it's not the same."

"I know how you feel. Maybe I could have avoided some of the burns on my hands if I didn't get so up close and personal with my food."

They were both glancing down at her hands smiled wryly. "I had a manicure and a pedicure on the weekend." She'd already removed the polish from her nails since it had chipped within a day. "The aesthetician thought I was a rock climber. When I told her what I do she said I have to start wearing gloves."

"I think your hands are beautiful." She was so surprised she would have pulled her hands out of his grasp had he not tightened his grip at the same moment. Holding them captive. She stared at him. "No one could like these hands."

"Someone else who works with their hands could."

And then he picked up one of her hands and pressed his lips against the hard calluses of her palms. The kiss was warm and moist and the sexiest thing that anyone had ever done to her in her whole entire life. He looked up as though gauging her response and whatever he saw on her face, he must've realized she was thrilled that someone should find her beaten up hands a thing of beauty. He kept his gaze on hers and lifted her hand once more. He kissed the bottom of her palm. He kissed the side edge that was more leather than skin. He slid the sleeve of her sweater a little higher exposing her wrist. "Any calluses up here?"

She was breathless, feeling the thrill go all through her. "I don't think so," she whispered.

"I'd better check." And then he pressed his lips to the most sensitive part of her wrist where her pulse was speeding up.

He kissed his way up towards her elbow pushing her sweater a little higher with each kiss. It was the slowest seduction she had ever experienced and yet the most intimate. When he got to her elbow and pressed his lips against the inner part where the skin was so sensitive she made a tiny sound, kind of a moan, and he abandoned the inside of her elbow and leaned forward, kissing her mouth.

She was so hungry for him, and she'd wanted this for so long, she threw her arms around him and kissed him back with every fiber of her being. She pushed her calloused hands into his hair, traced the shape of his head, ran her fingers down over his shoulders, over his back, pressing herself against him until something like a growl came out of his throat.

"Dinner," he said suddenly, "is going to be delayed."

He turned things down on the stove and then, to her shock, he bent down and scooped her up and into his arms. She felt like Cinderella, Scarlett O'Hara, and Marguerite Chance all rolled into one. He carried her as though she weighed no more than a feather, pounding up the stairs with her even as she clung on with her arms around his neck and a giggle of excitement travelling through her. They'd never made the tour upstairs and she discovered dimly that his room was very simple. Very him. He deposited her on top of his navy blue duvet and then pulled back to look down at her. "This okay?" He asked, suddenly looking uncertain. After his commanding Rhett Butler routine, she loved that moment of doubt.

"Oh it is very much okay." She reached up, grabbed his hands, and pulled him down on top of her. "So very much okay." And then the pair of them discovered how much pleasure two sets of scarred and callused hands could give.

They ate dinner much later. She wore an old pair of his athletic sweatpants and a T-shirt advertising a Greek restaurant in Chicago. He'd marinated tofu and grilled it with eggplant and tomatoes and the flavors were so sublime she felt like she could hear the waves of the Aegean Sea, and the faint music of a bouzouki. There were potatoes roasted in lemon and spanakopita hand made by his mother, as well as baklava for dessert.

"What?" she asked, raising her brows. "Only one dessert?"

He leaned forward and kissed her swiftly. "When we go to my folks' place, you'll eat so much dessert you'll beg for mercy. My mother thinks we'll starve to death if we don't leave the table groaning in pain. Then she sends everybody home with so many leftovers you pretty much have to hire a truck to move them."

After they'd eaten their fill he said, "I don't want to be too forward, but will you stay the night?"

Seemed like things had roared from 'Oh, my gosh I'm not even in his league' to 'Do you want to stay the night?' way too fast and yet, when she looked into his eyes, she felt that everything was going to be okay. When he looked at her she didn't feel like a plain, earthy woman with calloused, rough hands. She felt lush and beautiful with battle scarred hands to be proud of.

However, she didn't want to make it too easy for him. She tilted her head and said, "I don't know. Are you as good at cooking breakfast as you are at cooking dinner?"

For answer he gave her a very wolfish grin and advanced on her slowly. "There's only one way to find out. And I should warn you, I cook a very big breakfast. I suggest we build up a good appetite."

Normally, she liked sleeping in her own bed and waking up in her own home. She didn't expect to sleep much at all and she didn't, but not because of the strange bed. He kept her awake by making love to her over and over again. Each time, she was convinced she couldn't experience any more pleasure, and each time he proved her wrong. When, at last, they turned over to sleep, she rested so comfortably in the curve of his body behind her. There was something about the heat of his belly against her back and his arm curled over her torso that made her feel cherished.

They slept late the next morning. She was lying languorously in his bed and they were drinking their first cup of coffee together.

She wasn't a big coffee drinker, but the way he made it, and served it in his big yellow and blue mugs, she liked the dark brew just fine.

He ran a hand over her breast idly. "What do you like to eat for breakfast? I should stock some things if we're going to make a regular habit of this."

She glanced up at him, feeling out of her depth. She wanted to say something sexy and sophisticated, but she was more interested in understanding how he saw their future together—if there was one. "Are we going to make this a regular habit?" She meant to sound provocative but really the words sounded yearning. He leaned over and kissed her softly with coffee flavored lips. "I sure hope so."

His lips moved south and soon he was nuzzling the sensitive slope of her breast when her cellphone rang.

"Ignore it," he mumbled.

She was only too glad to do so. She'd long ago determined that she was not the kind of woman who was going to be ruled by any sort of electronic device. She was one of the last people she knew to even get a cellphone. And, when a man as exciting as Alexei was putting his lips exactly where he was putting his lips right now, her phone took low priority.

When she finally got around to checking the message she saw that it was Iris who had called. She'd also sent a text: *CALL ME NOW!!!* She related this to Alexei, who was finishing the last of his now cold coffee. He said, "Do you want me to give you some privacy?"

She shook her head. "It's probably Mom driving her crazy. That's what most of our emergencies are."

But when Iris picked up the phone almost before it rang, she started speaking so fast and with such excitement in her voice that Marguerite actually couldn't decipher a single word. She said, "Slow down. What happened?"

She could hear the shuddering breath Iris dragged in and then her sister said, so slowly that it sounded as though she were reminding herself to say each word distinctly, "I had my scan this morning."

She'd been so caught up with her dinner with Alexei that she'd completely forgotten about the scan. "How did it go?" She reached out and grasped Alexei's hand.

"It went great. There wasn't one little heartbeat. There were two! We're having twins!"

She squealed with joy. "You must be so excited. How is Geoff taking the news?"

"He's pretty stunned, to be honest. We both are. But in a good way."

"Oh my gosh, I can barely take it in. This is such good news."

"There's more good news."

She squeezed Alexei's hand harder.

"We've set a date to get married."

Yes, yes, yes! "Oh, Iris. I am so happy for you both."

There was a giggle from the other end. "Geoff said, he might let me be a single mom of one kid, but no way he was going to let me be a single mom of two kids. He insisted on marriage."

She chuckled. "Very old-fashioned, but I approve."

"Me, too. Oh, Marguerite, I had no idea everything could work out like this. That I could end up getting everything I wanted. I'm so happy."

She felt a shiver of recognition in the words and firmly reminded herself to focus on Iris, not herself.

"Have you told Mom yet?"

"I wanted to tell you first. Geoff told me that he talked to you and you gave him some really good advice on how to handle me. And I just want you to know how much I appreciate you. I want you to be my bridesmaid. My maid of honor, in fact."

Her eyes filled with sentimental tears. "I am so thrilled and of course I accept. I can't wait. When's the wedding?"

"We want something small as soon as possible. I don't want anything fancy. A quiet celebration with our family and the people closest to us. We're thinking maybe the week after next."

"Wow. You don't let grass grow."

"I know. We need to work around Geoff's school schedule. We won't get much of a honeymoon but at least we'll get a few days away. Rose has a friend with a cousin who knows how to run a bakery, it turns out. I'm going to interview her and hopefully she can help out when I'm away. Dosana can keep an eye on her. If she works out, I'll offer her a job."

"I don't even know what to say I am so excited. It's like everything is falling into place."

"I know. Listen, I'm here, now. Come over. Okay? Just drop everything and come over. We'll drink tea and eat muffins and I'll sit and grow my babies."

Marguerite had news of her own but this didn't feel like the right time to share it. She felt a tiny stab of guilt as she said, "Give me a couple of hours. You need to tell Mom and Dad and that's going to take at least an hour. I'll be over this afternoon."

Sounding a little puzzled, Iris said, "Okay. Is there something you're not telling me?"

She glanced over at Alexei and couldn't help the grin of pure mischief that crossed her face. "Yes, there is."

Iris hadn't known her all her life not to be pretty smart where Marguerite was concerned. After a short pause, she said, "Marguerite Chance, are you in bed with a man?"

"I will talk to you later."

A purely evil laugh answered her. "I will want details. Juicy, Technicolor, nothing left out, details."

"I'm hanging up now. Congratulations again."

"Thanks. Love you."

"Love you back. And my nieces and nephews. See you soon."

Alexei ran his hand through her hair. He didn't say anything, just gave her a moment to digest the news. She felt happy and intimate and delighted to have someone to share that news with, other than a rescue cat. "Iris and Geoff are having twins, and getting married in a couple of weeks. She wants me to be her maid of honor."

He leaned over and kissed her. "Of course she does. You'll be a perfect maid of honor."

She snuggled against his chest feeling warm and alive and happy. His words rumbled against her ear where it was pressed against his skin when he said, "I was hoping to spend the day with you. But it sounds like you need to go to your sister."

It was a beautiful thing to know he wanted to spend all day with her, even if it was to plan a cookbook, and that he understood she needed to be with her sister right now. She said, "I do have time, however, for breakfast."

He glanced at her quizzically. "Are you sure you worked up enough of an appetite?"

She sighed and stretched in pure bliss. "If I develop any more of an appetite I won't be able to walk down the stairs."

He gave her a resounding smack on the lips and then jumped out of bed naked and so mesmerizing she couldn't tear her eyes away. "You are so beautiful," she told him.

He turned to look at her, his expression tender. "You are."

THIRTEEN

AFTER DRESSING IN last night's clothes she tried to tame the tangle of her hair with his brush which was lying on top of his scarred wooden dresser. Beside it was a ceramic dish where he obviously tossed his change when he emptied his pockets at the end of the day. A scrap of paper, torn from a notebook, sat among the scatter of quarters and dimes. Originally folded, the paper had opened so she could read the message. It said, *Heidi*, then a phone number. After the phone number, Heidi had written, "Your girlfriend's a lucky gal, but I can be discreet. Call me," and punctuated her message with a hand-drawn heart.

She stood staring at the scrap of paper. That long-ago night in the Australian bar came back to her, when she'd found out Tim was cheating. She could hear that woman's voice in her head. "Darl, a man like him is a gift." Of course every woman wanted him. It wasn't his fault he was gorgeous and sexy.

His pockets were probably stuffed with scraps of paper bearing phone numbers.

But he hadn't tossed Heidi in the trash. And the word girlfriend jumped out at her like a broken heart.

She brushed her hair slowly, trying to still her racing heart.

When she got downstairs to the kitchen, she saw sunlight streaming in the big windows of his kitchen filling it with cheerful light.

He was so easy in his movements, as casual as though he had new women in his bed all the time. "Do you want to have another cup of coffee and watch me work? Or do you want to be my sous chef this morning?"

"If you don't mind, I'd like to watch the master at work."

"I can do that. What's your pleasure?"

"Why don't you surprise me?" She wanted to ask him about the girlfriend and the Heidis in his world, but she felt the need of a quiet space to think first. It was as though a brick sat in her chest, stopping the words coming out. She'd find her center, meditate, and then decide how to handle her feelings for Alexei. For now, she concentrated on holding it together until she was alone and could think.

He crossed to his fancy espresso machine to pour another cup for each of them and said, with his back turned, "That's what I like about the beginning of a new relationship. Everything's a surprise."

New relationship? One among how many? When she'd let herself be swept away by her passion last night, she'd kept it firmly in her mind that this was a fling. A night of no-strings sex with the most amazing, drool-worthy, exciting man she'd ever known, whose beauty almost hurt her to look at, but she hadn't realized until this morning what a mistake she was making. Everything about him screamed player from his looks to the way he charmed the women who swarmed to his food truck. She wondered if his girlfriend had any idea what he was really like? Was she as naïve as Marguerite had been with Tim?

Then she reasoned that people using a word like relationship gave it many different definitions. Maybe his idea of this relationship was that they would write a cookbook together and while she was convenient, and they were working closely together, it made perfect sense for them to be friends-with-benefits.

But she wanted a man of her own, who was exclusively hers and hers forever. Till-death-do-us-part forever. As she sat in that cheerful kitchen watching Alexei prepare her an omelet, giving her tips as he did so, she acknowledged that she craved kind of love that Iris and Geoff had, the kind of love her parents had.

How did they do that? Men like Alex and Tim, talk to a woman using the words she wanted to hear and sound so convincing?

And why did she keep falling for men she could never have?

When she left Alexei she immediately retreated to her

cottage where she indulged in a long hot shower, then rubbed her body with soothing lavender body oil but as she rubbed the oil into her skin she kept thinking about all the times during the night that Alexei had touched her there and stroked her here. She cursed herself for a fool but it didn't stop the memories.

She walked outside, breathing in the cool air and bundled together a selection of autumn flowers. Time in the garden usually soothed her, but today she felt heartsick. She never should have trusted him, and triple never should have slept with him. Hadn't she been down this road before? Only this time, she couldn't run home with her broken, battered heart. She *was* home.

She tried to concentrate on Iris's happiness as she arranged the flowers in one of the many vases she'd collected over the years for her homegrown bouquets. She bought old vases at flea markets and yard sales and saved interesting bottles. After peering through a shelf full of glass and ceramic, she passed over a ceramic baby in a pram, thinking it was too early. Instead, she chose a fluted vase made of milky glass. She sorted through a bundle of dahlias and chrysanthemums, ranging in color from deep purple to pumpkin orange, some yellow daisies, a tangle of pink Japanese Anemones and deep blue spikes of salvia, spicy with the smell of autumn. She trimmed stems and placed the blooms one by one, finding harmony as she pulled together different colors and sizes. After a while, she found the jumble of her thoughts beginning to settle as well. She didn't achieve the harmony of her flower arrangement, but at least she settled enough that she could show a calm face to her nosy family.

She drove over to Iris's house to find that she was not the first one there. In fact, she recognized several of the vehicles parked on the road out front. News travelled fast in the Chance family.

There was no point knocking on the door; she could hear the voices and laughter and excitement even from the porch. She took a moment to take in the sounds and just be grateful for this crazy, wacky family she was a part of and the joy that was ahead for them all with the new babies on the way.

She pushed open the door, hung her coat on one of the hooks in the hallway, picked up her bouquet and made her way into the main room, which in Iris's house was a kitchen-den combo. Iris sat in the two-seater sofa, surrounded by both parents and a selection of siblings. Geoff sat beside her, holding her hand in a way that suggested to Marguerite he had been in that same position for a while. Geoff was a man who made Iris happy, and exactly the kind of guy you wanted in a crisis, but Marguerite got the feeling, when her sister glanced up at her, that she was feeling a little overwhelmed. Her mom and dad were perched on the hearth in front of the fireplace, also holding hands, and sitting so close that at first glance they seemed to be one body rather than two. Neither of them seemed to even notice the handholding. They'd been doing that as long as she could remember.

Cooper, sitting on the floor, had a baby-naming book open and was throwing out likely names. "Jedediah Josephat has a nice ring to it."

Paisley shook her head at him. "The twins are girls. I know it."

When she caught sight of Marguerite and the flowers, Iris jumped up. Geoff said, "You sit, honey. I'll get them."

Iris was shaking her head already before she said, quite firmly, "No, that's okay. I'll do it."

She came into the kitchen and the sisters embraced. "I am so happy for you," Marguerite said. "I knew it would happen. I knew it."

"I can't believe it. I was scared I'd never have one baby. Now I'm having twins!"

Iris fussed over the flowers, touching and moving them slightly as though she were going to rearrange them when they both knew the arrangement was perfect and she just needed something to do with her hands. Marguerite said, "Feeling a little overwhelmed?"

"A little. Our family's great but, you know."

Iris didn't need to know the bad part, not when she was flying so high, so she stuck with part of the truth. "It was the most amazing night I've ever experienced in my entire life."

Her sister closed her eyes briefly, leaning back against the counter. "Details. I need details."

She shook her head. "Not here. Not now."

"Okay. I would just like to talk about anything

right now apart from babies, scans, and wedding details. It's all too much. There's a reason people usually get married first, and then have kids. You can only take on one huge project at a time." She glanced into the den where Cooper and Paisley were arguing over Adelaide and Sophie. Jack and Daphne were both laughing and Geoff looked as though he could play the baby-naming game all day long.

"Do you want me to get them out of here? Confiscate that book from Cooper? What can I do?"

Iris glanced over at the laughing group. "No. It's fine. I just needed a moment."

Marguerite looked at the chunk of her family sitting there and said, "Every baby should come into a family with this much love."

"With two babies? We're going to need all the help we can get."

"You said you maybe found a helper for the bakery?"

"Rose has a good friend who just got married. Apparently, she has a cousin, Kimberley, who used to work in a bakery. She's got some kind of training. They're supposed to be getting an email, a phone number or something. She lives in Portland but I get the feeling she's looking for something a bit quieter."

"That's great, it'll make your life a lot easier. And now that you're growing two babies instead of one, I tend to think Geoff's right, and you need to rest more."

Iris dropped her voice to a near whisper. "God knows I love that man, but if he doesn't stop trying to wrap me up in cotton wool and pamper me all day long I'm going to smack him upside the head with a frying pan."

She tried to bite back her smile but couldn't. "Don't forget he's overwhelmed too. It's his way of telling you he loves you and he wants to be there for you and the babies."

"I know. And I'm fully aware that I'm being a complete bitch. But, I figure with the number of hormones I've got running around my body, I'm allowed to be the Queen of the Bitches."

"Damn straight. And I am here to serve your majesty."

Alexei felt like his world was damn near perfect. His business was taking off, he had an interesting side hustle with the cookbook, and most of all, he had an amazing woman in his life. His night with Marguerite hadn't been planned. He'd followed, spontaneously, what had felt right. He was certain she had been on the same page with him. Nothing could have prepared him for the way she had made him feel. He loved her responsiveness when he touched her, her pleasure in her body and frank enjoyment of sex. The way she'd felt in his arms as they were drifting off to sleep and he could feel her heart beating beneath the breast he held cupped in his hand, the scent of her hair. He liked everything about her from her commitment to her business and the way she grew her food to the way she made him feel. She was such a relaxing person to be around. He was aware that he was always moving, always multi-tasking, but she had the rare gift of focus. When they were together, he knew he had all her attention. She wasn't checking her Facebook while he was talking, or fiddling with her hair or twitching.

Having watched her get ready to go to her parents' place for dinner, after the fall fair, he'd liked that she didn't take half a day to get her makeup just right or try on seven outfits before selecting one. If she had a fashion style, it was a combination of Earth mother and hippie chick. She seemed drawn to natural fabrics and soft, well-worn jeans. They suited her natural beauty. His mother was right. And it cost him something to admit that his mother was right, Marguerite wasn't the conventional beauty of air brushed celebrities and anorexic models. Hers was the kind of beauty that was celebrated in his home country. It was in the rounded shape of her face, the full mouth, the depth in her eyes, her luxurious hair as well as her womanly curves. His mother might be a pain in the ass in many ways, but she was smart.

He wasn't a bit surprised when his mom called. "I like that girl. The one you had for dinner. She's good for you."

He couldn't help but shake his head. "Mama, you saw her for five minutes."

"I have eyes, me. I saw the way you looked at her. I also saw the way she looked at you." And she chuckled softly. "Besides, she said she wants children."

"You bulldozed that poor woman into a corner, what was she supposed to say? Anyway, she said she likes children, not that she plans to have dozens with me so that you can get your grandma fix."

"I've been on this earth a lot longer than you, plus I'm a woman, we always see more. Trust me when I tell you that girl is good for you."

He didn't want to admit to his mother how right she was. But he knew in his heart that Marguerite was right for him on many levels. The trouble was, Marguerite didn't seem to feel the same way about him. She'd made a couple of comments that morning over breakfast that had suggested she was not looking for anything serious. That surprised him as he'd believed she would take her relationships pretty seriously.

He was also disappointed. At this point in his life, and he would never admit this to his mother, he was looking to get serious. At heart, he supposed he was his mother's son and his father's son. His dreams and ambitions had never been big. He had a job he enjoyed, something that he was good at which made him proud. He felt established in life and deep down he knew he was ready to settle down with the right woman, God willing to have a few of those kids his mother wanted so badly, become a stalwart member of the community.

Sure, he was never going to set the world on fire,

or save lives the way his brother Matt did, but he was fine with that. If he could feed people good food, keep alive the traditions of his homeland, and make enough money to live comfortably, he was happy.

The cookbook was an unexpected bonus. Not so much because he thought he would make money off it, but because it allowed him to see Marguerite in a very nonthreatening way. The irony wasn't lost on him that he, who had been forced to change phones several times in order to avoid women who were a lot more interested in him than he was in them was now looking for excuses to phone the woman he genuinely was interested in.

Of course, he'd never been under any illusions that those women had seen him for who he was. It was the Adonis curse. But, when Marguerite looked at him, he felt that she really saw him. Maybe that was why she was so special. She saw below the surface to the man he was inside, and he was arrogant enough to think that he could see her too. So, for now they'd work on a cookbook and he'd do something he'd had to do very little in his life—he'd work at wooing a woman.

He picked up his phone and, under his startled gaze, the thing started to ring. His heart jackknifed in his chest when he read on his call display the word Chance. He answered so quickly he nearly dropped the damn phone. "Hey there, I was just thinking about you," he said, feeling warm all over that Marguerite was calling.

A beat of silence that was too long for comfort had

him cursing himself for a fool. And then a voice that was definitely not Marguerite's and laced with humor said, "I'm glad to hear it. I was thinking about you, too, which is why I got my mother to give me your phone number. This is *Iris* Chance." He noted that she put an emphasis on the word Iris as though he hadn't already figured out he was not speaking to the delectable Marguerite but to her sister. "We met at the fall fair. I had one of your souvlakis and it was amazing."

Since she'd brought the dessert to Daphne and Jack's dinner, he'd sampled one of her pies and found it excellent. He said, "And you bake a mean pie."

She laughed softly. "Mutual admiration among foodies. That's a good start."

"What can I do for you?"

"Well, as you may have heard, I'm getting married."

He hadn't said anything because, even though Marguerite had told him that Iris was pregnant and getting married, he wasn't officially supposed to know these things. Now he had the news from the bride's mouth, he figured it was okay to say, "Congratulations."

"Thanks. I'm also pregnant. Which is making things just a little bit more complicated."

"I can imagine. That's a lot of good news to absorb at once."

"Exactly! Thank you for understanding. Normally, of course, I would cater my whole wedding myself.

But, I have to be realistic. I can only handle the wedding cake."

He didn't say anything but in his mind building a wedding cake had to be a huge feat. With a wedding to plan and a business to run and a couple of babies to grow this woman clearly had a lot of energy.

"I was wondering whether you would consider catering my wedding?"

He was about to refuse as he did not do catering. When he'd drawn up his business plan he had decided early on that he would stay narrow in his focus. Food trucks worked for him. He cooked food for the people, and he handed it out to them. He didn't aspire to own a restaurant. He didn't want white cloths and crystal glasses and wine lists getting in the way of what, in Greece, was basically street food.

He never wanted to get into the catering industry despite the many requests he'd received. However, he knew that Marguerite was going to be in the wedding party and, lovestruck fool that he was, he could work out that if he catered the wedding he'd have more reasons to see a lady he had come to like very, very much.

He wouldn't stray too far from his principles, however, not even for Marguerite. So he said, "I don't do a lot of catering. And I wouldn't be in a position to change my menu too much."

"No. I don't want you to. That's what I loved about your food. It's delicious but not fancy. We are planning the world's most casual wedding. The reception will be at my parents' place, which is hardly fancy as you know. But it's got plenty of room and if the weather's nice people can spill outside. I want our guests to walk around with small bites of delicious food, exactly the kind of stuff that you serve from your truck. Maybe with some smaller bites."

"What's your date?"

"Really? ASAP. I would like to be able to get married on the Saturday two weeks from now. But I could stretch it to three depending on your schedule."

He thought briefly. He had casual staff who could take over his main truck. He'd bring all his food up in one of the smaller trucks. "Two weeks is not a problem. How many people are you expecting?"

"We're trying to keep it to fifty. But, we have the big family and a lot of friends. So fifty is probably going to be seventy."

Mentally, he decided to cook enough food for a hundred. He could already see this was the kind of wedding that was going to creep up in numbers. Daphne and Jack Chance being two of the most social people he'd ever met and pillars of their small community, he suspected Iris was going to have a larger wedding than she planned. He said, "I'll draw up a sample menu and email it to you. I'll only charge for the cost of the ingredients."

She started to protest but he cut her off firmly. "My brother's marrying your sister, that makes us practically family. Besides, I'm working on a cookbook with Marguerite. We can try out some of our new recipes on your guests if that's okay."

"I feel awful. I never thought that your brother would want you to cater *his* wedding. Will he be upset do you think, if I ask you to cater my wedding first?"

He couldn't stop the laugh that shook him. "My brother? You think my fancy assed Doctor brother is going to have his wedding catered from a Greek food truck? I'll bet you fifty bucks that my brother and your sister hire the most expensive hotel in Portland and we dine on tiny, very expensive things that have been flown in from other parts of the world, which we will down with expensive, vintage wines dragged out of somebody's private cellar."

Iris's spurt of laughter was surprisingly like Marguerite's. "They are well matched, aren't they? I won't take that bet, I'm too sure you're right. Okay, then, if you're sure, I accept your very generous offer. Thank you."

"No problem."

He jotted down a few ideas for a sample menu. A lot of what he was imagining were items he already cooked but on a smaller scale. He'd keep it simple, scale down his spanakopitas, cook up cocktail-size skewers of souvlaki, Greek lemon potatoes that could be served with toothpicks. A variety of dips with pita bread and small chunks of feta done in different marinades. And big bowls of olives. He'd serve his Tomatoes Marguerite if she could get him some good tomatoes.

FOURTEEN

HE HAD PLANNED to call Marguerite anyway, and now he was glad that Iris had forestalled him because instead of phoning Marguerite with some vague idea of getting together, he now called with a definite purpose. He liked the way she answered the phone. She had to know it was him since she had his number programmed into her cell phone but she still answered, "Hello?"

So he went along with the idea that she didn't actually know who was calling and said, "Marguerite. It's Alexei."

"I was pretty sure it was, but I like to be absolutely certain."

He thought she was charmingly old-fashioned that she didn't trust call display to tell her the truth and then he was forcibly reminded of his boneheaded move earlier when he had answered his ringing phone. He said, "You're smart. A little while ago I answered my phone thinking it was you, and it was your sister."

"Rose called you?"

He figured that was a fair assumption to make since Rose was currently engaged to his brother and, he supposed, when a woman had as many sisters us Marguerite did it was easy to get them mixed up. He said, "No. Iris."

"Iris called you?"

"She did. And I thought it was you, so I picked up the phone and told her I was thinking about her."

There was silence for a moment and he knew she was taking in the fact that he'd been thinking about. "That's nice," she said softly. And then, "But what did Iris want?"

"She wants me to cater her wedding."

"But you don't do catering."

"I don't normally do catering. But, like I told her, her sister's marrying my brother, so we're practically family. Besides, I was thinking you and I could use this as an excuse to work up some recipes for the cookbook. What do you think?"

"You'd really cater my sister's wedding?"

"I've already agreed to do it."

"If you had any idea how she's been stressing over the catering... She wanted to do the whole thing herself, for her to trust you to cater her wedding is a huge compliment to you. And for you to agree to do it is a huge relief to the rest of us. So, thank you."

He'd have preferred words of passion and promise, but he supposed gratitude was better than nothing. He said, "Don't be too grateful, you're getting involved in this too."

"Me? I can't cook anything."

"You can chop things and you can taste. Plus, we can start combining my recipes with what grows locally in abundance. Iris is getting married in two weeks. Would you have any time in the next few days? Say, tomorrow?"

"Tomorrow. Um, yes. Of course."

"Great." He felt the warmth of anticipation simply knowing he would see her tomorrow. "I'll be finished work at four. Why don't you come to my place around five. Bring some samples of whatever you've got fresh right now. We'll play."

"Play?" She sounded suspicious as though what he had in mind involved very adult games. Naturally, that put pictures in his head that immediately made him want to do nothing but play adult games with her all night. However, he forced himself to laugh and said, "Sure. That's how we invent new recipes. We take different ingredients and play. It's an adventure. You'll see."

"Can I ask you something?"

"Anything."

"Do you have a girlfriend?"

"What? Of course not. We just had sex, why would you even ask?"

There was a pause as though she were contemplating what to say, while he tamped down anger that she would even ask him such a thing after what they'd shared. "I wasn't snooping, honest I wasn't, but there was a note on your dresser from a woman named Heidi. It said something about her being discreet since you have a girlfriend."

He didn't remember any such note, but his stomach sank anyway. "It's the curse," he said finally. "Women sometimes come on to me. It's been happening since I was thirteen." He could go on for hours about the embarrassing situations he'd been thrown into by eager girls and women. "The girlfriend was Matt's idea."

"What?"

"I don't have a girlfriend, but Matt said that when a girl makes a pass, I should tell her I have a girlfriend. Saves everyone's feelings."

"So, the girlfriend is a lie?"

He didn't like how bad that sounded. "A white lie so no one's feelings get hurt."

"And you didn't call Heidi?"

"I don't even know who Heidi is."

"Oh."

"Are we good?"

There was another long pause, and he held his breath until she said, "Yes, we're good. I'll see you tomorrow."

He pretty much bounced through the lunch rush next day, joking with patrons, flirting with women who were old enough to be his mother, and treating anyone in his general age range as though he were their brother. He left Melissa to do the final cleanup and close up so he was able to get away a little early. He bolted home, grabbed a long hot shower, shaved and put on clean clothes. He wasn't a huge slob but he took a few minutes to make sure the clothes he'd worn were tidily stowed in the laundry hamper, and that he'd picked up any clutter. He did not need to check his kitchen, because he always kept his kitchen spotless and it was the most well-organized room in his house.

Even though this was a working gig, he put music on softly. Since they would be working through the evening, he set about preparing a big, beautiful salad which he would serve with a fresh loaf of crusty bread he had picked up on his way home.

Then, reminding himself that he invited her over for work and not play, he pulled up the sample menus on his computer and started making notes.

When his doorbell rang, right on the dot of five o'clock, he was more than ready.

He walked to the front door, opened it and she stood there, her long hair like shadows of midnight hanging over her shoulders, her blue eyes dark and full of mystery. When she saw him her lips parted slightly and he felt that she was remembering, as he was, the depth of their passion the last time they had seen each other.

He meant to say something casual like, "Come in." The words stuck in his throat. She opened her mouth as though she were going to say something equally innocuous and nothing came from her mouth either. For a long moment they stood there, gazes glued to each other, and then he took a step forward, and she took a step forward, and without ever a word being spoken she threw herself into his arms at exactly the same moment he pulled her in. All he could think about was the press of her body against his, the feel of her mouth hungry, demanding, moving against his. He turned them and managed to kick the door shut behind them with his foot.

They fell into a routine, after that. She'd come over, they'd play with food, put a local twist on one of his signature recipes, and each time he slipped a morsel of food into her mouth, or she argued with him over the choice of wording, it was like foreplay. Their nights always ended in passion. He'd never enjoyed a woman, or a project, more. The cookbook provided the perfect excuse for them to see each other every day, but he knew that he'd have wanted to see her every day no matter what. He was falling for Marguerite Chance, and falling hard. He liked to think he saw his feelings reflected back at him, but he wasn't certain enough to declare himself.

Not yet. Didn't want to scare the woman away. So, he wooed her with food, and she wooed him, whether she knew she was doing it or not, with her easy smile, her passion, her commitment to her work, and the open, loving way she gave of herself at night.

He doubted anyone but his mother knew that he was a romantic at heart. But he was. And with his brother engaged to Marguerite's sister, and another sister getting married in less than a week, he felt like love and marriage were all around him. He'd always been impatient, and never more so than now. He'd found the woman he wanted to spend the rest of his life with, and he felt a strong urge to shout his feelings to the world!

Or at least whisper them into Marguerite's ear.

While he was passing a craftsman jewelry store, a silver ring caught his eye and made him think of the way her silver rings sparkled on Marguerite's hands when she was gesturing, or when she ran them over his body. On impulse, he went in and bought the ring, thinking how pretty it would look on her hand. It wasn't diamonds, not enough to scare her off, but he felt that giving a woman a ring was his way of saying he was serious.

He'd do it Thursday, he decided. Iris's wedding was Saturday. Maybe he was crazy, but he wanted to tell Marguerite his feelings at least before Saturday.

On Thursday, he was in a great mood as he arrived at his food truck. Maybe because he was so focused on what he was going to say that night, he wasn't paying much attention to what was under his nose. Melissa was already there, as he'd expected, everything was opened up and she was chopping onions. When he heard her sniffing, he assumed the onions were to blame.

"Hey," he said.

"Hey," she replied without turning.

They worked side-by-side mostly in silence, with the ease of people who had worked together for a long time. He noted that she didn't have her earphones on today blasting out alternative music that only she could hear. When he finally caught a glimpse of Melissa's face he realized it wasn't onions making her sniff, but a full on cold. Her eyes were red and her face blotchy. He said, "Are you okay to work here today?"

She blinked then nodded and turned quickly away. They got busy and he didn't have time to worry about sending her home. And then, as usually happened, there was a lull. He'd been doing everything mechanically today, from cooking to serving, even his joking with the customers was the kind of thing he could do with his brain already fast-forwarded to later. He was nervous. He was nervous about tonight, and what he was going to say to Marguerite and whether it was too soon to tell her he loved her, and what she might say back. Was the ring too much, too soon?

Melissa and he didn't have a close, personal relationship, but they'd worked together for a couple of years now, and she was a woman. He turned to her, in the middle of wiping down the counter, and asked, wet rag in one hand, "Melissa, can I ask you something?"

She glanced up warily. "Sure."

He said, "It's kind of personal, but I need some advice."

"Sure. But don't expect an answer."

That's what he liked about Melissa. She always said exactly what she thought. Plus, she wasn't remotely interested in him, which made her an easy working companion. "Okay." He wiped down the counter a little more, to give him time. Finally, he said, "You know Marguerite?"

She glanced at him, her reddened eyes narrowing slightly. "Marguerite, as in the produce lady?"

"Yeah. Her. Well, I've been seeing her for a few weeks now."

"I figured something was putting you in a good mood. Had to be a woman."

"The thing is, I'm crazy about her. Do you think it's too soon to tell her I love her?"

Melissa stared at him for a moment as though he'd spoken a completely foreign language. He replayed his words in case he'd been so excited he'd spoken in Greek, but he was pretty sure he'd said the words in English. Then, to his shock and utter dismay, his prep cook's eyes filled with tears and spilled over down her face. She put her hands up to cover her emotional outbreak and then turned away mumbling, "I'm sorry."

All thoughts of Marguerite were forgotten. He dropped the damp rag and came up behind Melissa. "Hey," he said gently. "It's okay." She was sobbing now, noisy dragging soul-sucking sobs. They'd never been the hugging types, but he went on instinct and pulled her in against his chest. Leaning out with one hand he pulled the shutter down, effectively closing the truck to give her some privacy. Then he began to rub his hand gently up and down her back.

After a few minutes, the painful crying eased and she raised her head. "I just got dumped. Like, last night. I just, you talked about love, and I — I, I feel like I'm never going to get there."

He lifted her chin so he could look her right in the eye. "You will. Any woman who was stupid enough to dump *you* didn't deserve you in the first place." And then, when she gave a very little smile, he leaned forward and gave her a brotherly peck on the lips.

At that moment, the door opened and Marguerite stepped inside. Melissa gave a little gasp of horror and pulled away from him, turning away, probably so that Marguerite wouldn't see her tear stained face. He shifted his body a little, helping block her from Marguerite's view. And said, "Hi. I wasn't expecting to see you until tonight."

"Obviously," she said. She didn't exactly spit the word but it was clear right away that she had witnessed the world's most innocent kiss and misunderstood it. She dumped a box of something green on the floor. "I guess I should've called first." And then she turned and headed outside again.

He followed her. "Marguerite!" He said to her rapidly retreating back. "Hold up!"

"I don't think so." And she kept right on walking.

He couldn't believe she wouldn't stop and hear him out. "Come on, would you please let me explain what's going on?"

He followed her, jumped down off the back of the

truck and jogged so he could catch up. "Hey."

Now she turned and he could see the blaze of anger in her eyes and a cold, disdainful expression pinching her mouth. "I have eyes. I could see perfectly well what was going on." And then she let out a sound of fury. "I am so stupid. I keep believing your stories about women hitting on you and trusting that you aren't interested, but you weren't brushing off Melissa. You were kissing her! I thought you were different. I believed in you."

He was starting to feel a little hot under the collar. "You can trust me. Nothing is going on with me and Melissa."

"I think our definitions of nothing are a little different. I get that you can't help it, with your looks, you can have every woman you want, so obviously you help yourself like we're some endless box of chocolates. But I can't do this. I can't be with a man I don't trust."

He was so stunned he felt as though she had slapped him. After all they'd shared, did she really think he'd cheat on her? He shook his head, "You really think I'm that guy?"

"Oh do not pull that," and then she lowered her voice and shook her finger, "'I did not have sexual relations with that woman' crap. I don't have time for it."

A family of four approached the truck, puzzled, looking at the closed shutter on an otherwise obviously operating food truck and then turned to him. They were regulars and they knew him. Tom, the dad, said, "Hey Alex, you open for business?"

He was about to ask them to give him five minutes when Marguerite said, "Oh don't you worry, he's always open for business." And then she stomped off.

This time, he let her go.

FIFTEEN

NO ONE COULD believe it, but Iris's faith that she would have sunshine for her October wedding day turned out to be well-placed. Marguerite rose that morning with the sun and had the pleasure of watching the first rays of sunlight bathe her garden and the surrounding fields.

The cottage had been designated bridal preparation HQ and she was all ready with pins and her sewing kit, a curling iron and extra makeup, everything she could think of that a bride or bridesmaid might need at the last minute. But it was early, so she took her time following her usual routine that always calmed her. She'd retreated inside for her yoga the last few days, but this morning was surprisingly warm. She stepped out onto the porch sniffing the crispness of fall in the air, like a juicy apple.

She did her usual sun salutations and a few extra relaxation poses but the relaxation simply wasn't happening. It wasn't that she was nervous about Iris's wedding. She was as joyful as a sister could be for a woman who has found her perfect mate, and is celebrating their union before all their friends and family. No, her edginess was about having to see Alexei today.

They hadn't spoken since she'd caught him in a lip-lock with Melissa. Not that she'd have listened to his lame explanations if he'd bothered to try and make any, but after following her out of the food truck, he hadn't tried to contact her again. Really, what was there to say?

He'd arrive soon, to set up for the catering. She had to see him at the wedding and she didn't know how to handle her feelings. She'd never been sophisticated about male-female relationships. She loved simply and maybe too easily and so she set herself up to get her heart broken. Not that it was entirely Alexei's fault, of course. She had only needed to take one look at his gorgeous, too-perfect-to-be-real face and body and realize that any woman who fell for him was going to be in trouble.

Once more, she reflected on the lesson she'd learned in Australia and she had to concede she'd fallen into the same trap again. She couldn't expect a man who looked like Alex to stick to one woman. Why would he? He could have any woman he wanted. Well, most of them anyway. Not her, though. Not ever again. She was going to update her dating profile and specify No Good-looking Men!

She needed to pull herself out of this bad mood and focus, not on herself, and her bruised and slightly cracked — oh, who was she kidding her broken heart, but on Iris, who was celebrating a very special day and did not need a self-involved sniveling sister to spoil it. Having given herself that rousing pep talk, she cooked a nourishing omelet for breakfast and sat there staring at it.

Memories, like movie scenes, ran through her head. Alexei making her breakfast, looking at her in that intimate way. The way they'd laughed and the incredible strength of connection she had felt with him. The truth was, she had never felt anything like that with Tim back in Australia. He'd been more of a fantasy than a man. The sort of guy who reminded her of a movie star. And, maybe she had cast herself as his leading lady for as long as that movie had run. Those credits had rolled long ago and she'd moved on. When she compared her feelings then with her feelings now, she wondered if she had really made the same mistake twice. She had a feeling that the answer was no.

She'd gone to Alexei with her eyes open and in truth she hadn't even tried to hold herself back from falling for him. It wasn't even his over-the-top good looks that had appealed to her. It was something more. The intense way they both felt about food. The arguments that they could have over organic versus local for instance. They were both passionate in their opinions but also respected each other's judgment and that they wouldn't always agree. They never ran out of things to talk about. And when he looked at her, she had believed he genuinely cared.

She forced herself to dig into her breakfast, knowing she'd be busy and unable to eat properly for several hours. The omelet was better because he'd shown her a few tips, such as starting with the eggs at room temperature, and cooking the eggs, only eggs, no added water or milk, in butter. He'd shown her how to jiggle the pan and swirl the spatula to create the perfect consistency.

Great. Now she could cook something and her new skill only made her sad.

She missed him, not only as the man who'd made her feel things she'd never felt before but as her friend. Her colleague.

She heard the rumbling of his truck grinding along the gravel lane beside her cottage. She tried to remain in her seat at her kitchen table, but it was hopeless. She rose and crept to the window and watched as Alexei's food truck rumbled past. She glimpsed the side of his head through the truck window and then, almost as though he couldn't help it anymore that she could, he turned his head and glanced towards her cottage.

She didn't think he could see her standing back and out of the way, but she felt as though their gazes connected and she felt such a searing pain in her chest that she had to put her hand there for a moment. And then he rumbled on, the bright colors painted on the side of his truck turning into a blue and yellow blur.

After she'd cleaned up her breakfast things, she indulged herself a little. Since she had lots of time, she drew herself a bath, pouring in a bubbling oil scented with patchouli and rose. She'd suffered a manicure and pedicure yesterday in honor of today, but her hands were hopeless. Pretty, pink tips didn't match the hard calluses that no amount of cream or paraffin treatments could remove.

She sat there in the bath looking at them, glistening up at her from the wet and remembered the way Alexei had kissed those rough calluses and made her feel as though that part of her was beautiful. She put her hands down so hard the water splashed up. She had to stop this. She had to stop this infantile moping over a relationship that had ended almost before it began.

The worst part was that he hadn't even looked guilty when he'd come running after her. He'd gazed at her as though she were the one with the problem. He'd told her to trust him. And she wanted to. But how could she? When every time she turned around there was another beautiful woman hanging off his arm or drooling at his feet. Or kissing him in the hastily shuttered food truck!

She tried not to think of Alexei as she finished her bath and shaved all the bits of her that needed shaving and rubbed her body with a beautiful almond-scented cream. Iris had not insisted that they all go to a hairdresser and get big fancy hairdos for which she was very grateful. She put hot rollers in and set her own hair in long, loose curls. There had not been time to order bridesmaid dresses, so the four of them, Iris and Rose and Marguerite and Paisley had gone shopping.

It had been Rose's idea for each of them to choose a different dress in one of the fall colors. Rose picked a stunning green number, Paisley's dress was rich antique gold and for her they found a deep purple that brought out the color in her eyes. "It's too tight," she'd complained as they were trying on dresses at Nordstrom.

Rose, who knew more about fashion than the rest of them put together, had scoffed. "It's time you showed off your curves. This is fabulous on you." She'd glanced at Iris who nodded and gave a thumbs up. It was hard to argue with Rose when she used that tone. Later, when she protested about Rose's bossiness to Iris, the bride said, "I know. But she was right. You look fantastic in that dress."

As she slipped into the purple which she were over sexy underwear that no one but she knew she owned, she had to admit, Rose was right.

Maybe it was because there was so little time to plan this wedding, or maybe the stars had aligned. But, they'd found all the dresses and accessories in one afternoon. Iris tried on one dress that fit perfectly and she loved it. And each of the other bridesmaids found a dress almost as quickly.

She'd barely finished applying her makeup when she heard a commotion coming from outside. Girlish giggles and high-pitched conversations running over each other that could only be the women of her family. She smiled as she headed towards the door and opened it. A quartet of excited women tumbled in looking like as many fall leaves swirling.

Iris was the only one in jeans. She had left her dress here so there was no chance that Geoff would catch so much as a glimpse of his bride's gown before the wedding.

She'd spent last night in her childhood bed in her childhood home, and was terrified that Geoff might catch a glimpse of her or her gown before the wedding and some very superstitious bad thing might happen because of it. But, from the excited light in her eyes, Marguerite could see that her fears were behind her. She said, "Didn't I tell you? Didn't I tell you this was going to be a beautiful day?"

Marguerite smiled at her happiness. "You did. And you were right. I think when the sun smiles on your wedding day, that's a very good sign."

Five minutes later Daphne entered, carrying the box holding Iris's shoes and another box with her daughter's bouquet.

Since they were all pretty much ready, the three bridesmaids and the bride settled into Marguerite's couches. Iris was all made up, and she'd run into town this morning to have her hair styled in a soft updo.

Daphne set the things down on a handy table and then came forward. And then she stopped and simply stared at the four women.

Rose glanced up first at the abnormally quiet Daphne. "Mom? Are you all right?" Daphne was not a woman to stand silent for very long.

She nodded, and her eyes filled with tears. "I just had a moment, looking at you, and realizing how beautiful you all are, and how proud I am of every single one of you. Jack and I have done plenty of foolish things in our time, but each one of you children is such a blessing that it makes up for everything else."

There was a sudden blinking of five pairs of eyes. Rose said, "Mom, stop! You'll make us wreck our makeup."

They all laughed and blinked back their sudden emotion. Even so, they stood as though on a silent command and gathered around their mother where they indulged in a clingy group hug.

As Daphne wiped her eyes she said, "I'm allowed to cry. I haven't done my makeup yet. Besides, as the mother of the bride it's my right to cry. And I'm claiming it." She glared at them. "All day."

Iris stepped back and straightened her spine. "Well, I'm not crying. I've decided. This is the happiest day of my life and I am not going to shed a single tear."

Rose made a rude noise. "With those hormones rushing around your body like crazy? You'll be sobbing all day."

"Will not."

"Will so."

"Bets?"

Daphne stepped forward, laughing. She touched Iris's cheek. "You'll have a perfect day, whether you cry or you don't. I only want you to enjoy every minute. Geoff is a very special man. I almost think he deserves you."

Feeling that someone had to step up before Daphne had them all in tears again, Marguerite said, "Okay, let's get Iris into her dress and then we'll take some pictures. Mom? Are you dressing here or at your place?"

"Here. My dress is under there somewhere," she said, pointing vaguely to the pile of stuff she'd brought with her.

Iris had insisted she didn't want stiff, formal wedding photos so they'd decided to simply take snaps throughout the day. By the time they were all dressed and ready, the sound of snapping cameras and the selfie posing was so practiced they barely noticed. She imagined a lot of the images would end up deleted, but she liked the candid nature of grabbing these precious moments of Iris's big day.

Finally, they were all ready to go.

Daphne wore a sapphire blue dress and complained the second she slipped her feet into heels. "There's a reason I never wear heels," she groused, as Rose brushed blush onto her cheeks and Paisley worked the curling iron in her hair.

Daphne spent most of her life in jeans, work shirts and little or no makeup and still she was a very attractive woman. But get that woman in a decent dress, heels and made up and she was a knock out. "Wait until Dad sees you," Rose said as she stepped away. "He'll be drooling."

Iris turned to her mother. "One rule. No making out with Dad at my wedding."

They all giggled, Daphne hardest of all, for she and Jack had never been big on hiding their love from their kids. It had been mortifying when they were teenagers but now, Marguerite thought they all kind of liked the exuberant affection of their parents. But not, she privately agreed, at Iris and Geoff's wedding. "Somebody better tell Dad it's hands off until you're alone."

"Well, I'm not doing it," Daphne said, looking much younger than her fifty-six years.

"I'll do it," Rose said. They all nodded. Rose could get Jack to do anything and they all knew it. Especially Jack.

Iris and Geoff had chosen to be married in the small wooden United Methodist church in town, so Evan and Matt were acting as designated wedding chauffeurs. They arrived right on time. They'd both had their cars washed and each vehicle sported a big white bow. For a last minute affair, this wedding was surprisingly well organized.

Iris, Paisley and Daphne slipped into Matt's car while the remaining bridesmaids got into Evan's.

Both men jumped out to open the rear doors for their passengers, exactly like real chauffeurs. Evan had even acquired a chauffeur's cap from somewhere. "Ladies," he said in full formality. "I hope you enjoy your ride."

He helped them all into the car and they drove

decorously to the church where Iris would be married.

Daphne gave Iris one last hug and then walked into the church to take her place. Jack walked forward and said, "You girls look great." In his suit, he looked like a Grateful Dead groupie accidentally on stage with The Three Tenors. He'd had his beard trimmed, and his shoes shined, and as he held out his arm to Iris, he said, "Let's do this thing."

Since there wasn't a wedding co-ordinator, Rose gave the organist the high sign and the music changed to a pounded rendition of the wedding march.

Rose went first, followed by Paisley, and it was her turn. Marguerite had the perfect view of Geoff's face as he glimpsed his bride and the expression on his face brought a lump of emotion to her throat. The church seated eighty, but there were at least a hundred people squeezed into the pews. No one seemed to care about the overcrowding. She could feel the love coming from Geoff's colleagues and students, his family, and the Chance clan, Iris's friends and even some of her loyal customers who had turned up to help celebrate.

Maybe there was no such thing as a perfect wedding, but Marguerite thought that this one came pretty darned close. If there was an ache in her chest that her own love life was the opposite of Iris's, she tried to squelch it and focus on being happy for Iris.

SIXTEEN

AFTER THE CEREMONY, the celebrations moved to Jack and Daphne's back yard. As she mingled with the guests, most of whom she already knew, Marguerite tried to pretend that her heart rate wasn't elevated.

Alexei and Iris had planned out the food, but she'd felt part of the planning, since they'd talked recipes in that brief, wonderful time they'd been lovers and colleagues. The food stations were exactly where Iris had planned them, and the simple, colorful food was a huge hit with the guests, who walked around with small mismatched china plates laden with perfect bites of simple Greek food.

She refused to look in the general direction of the kitchen, never mind go in there. Alexei, she knew, was there. She could feel his presence as though there were an invisible lasso tied around her waist and he was tugging at it, so strongly did she feel the urge to go to him. He might even need help, not that she was exactly the most useful person in the kitchen, but she could chop and rinse and tidy with the best of them.

However, she was perfectly certain that he had Melissa there helping him with anything he needed. Food related or otherwise. Besides, Daphne, who had an embarrassing older woman's crush on him, would certainly be dashing in there to help. Never mind that this was her daughter's wedding.

She tried to snap herself out of such ungenerous thoughts. She pulled out one or two of the meditation techniques she'd learned through the years, but nothing worked. In the end, she took a deep breath and forced herself to walk forward into the main room. Just because Iris hadn't wanted a lot of fancy floral arrangements at her wedding, didn't mean that Marguerite hadn't used her talents to help decorate the large and somewhat shabby main living room of Daphne and Jack's house. She glanced around with pleasure at the tall vases bursting with fall colors: chrysanthemums ranging from a deep glorious purple to an antique gold color, dahlias and even a few late roses and boughs of autumn leaves that she found on their property. The look was whimsical, colorful and casual and it suited Iris and Geoff's wedding perfectly.

One of the large chrysanthemum heads looked as though it were nodding off for a nap, drooping untidily over the edge of the vase. She stepped forward and shuffled it to the back so its lack of dignity wouldn't be so obvious. Geoff, looking proud and happy and very formal in his dark blue suit came up to her and said, "Those are beautiful. They really change the atmosphere in here."

She laughed softly. "Let's face it, the Chance house is never going to be fancy or elegant, but it's got a certain lived-in charm."

He nodded. "I know this sounds crazy, but you can feel the happiness in here. It's like it oozes out of the walls or something."

"I've always felt that way, but I assumed it was because I grew up here. I mean, this is our family home, we celebrated birthdays and family dinners and now weddings and, in spite of some arguments and hard times, we've been a very happy family."

"Believe me, it's not just you. I'm not the most touchy-feely guy, but some houses, you walk into them and you can feel the unhappiness and the years of bickering. But the moment I first walked into this house, on Iris's birthday, last year, I felt the love."

She glanced up at him, teasing, "Are you sure the love was coming from the house? Or did it have anything to do with your infatuation with my cookie-baking, short-story-writing sister?"

He laughed and glanced down at his brand-new wedding ring as though surprised to find it there. "I guess you've got me there." He seemed as though he were about to say more, paused, pushed the wedding ring around his finger a little bit and then finally said, "I haven't had an opportunity to thank you yet. You gave me really good advice when I needed it and helped me find the way to talk to Iris. To convince her to set a date."

"You two are so in love with each other, it was

inevitable you would find your way. If I helped even a little bit then I'm glad. I'm also really happy to have you as a brother." She didn't even add the in-law part. One of the things she'd learned growing up in the Chance family where the kids were a mixture of purebred Chances and strays was that you didn't love people because you shared their DNA. What they shared was the bond of choosing to love and support each other. She had a feeling that Geoff made a very good addition to her family.

"And I couldn't imagine having a better sister than you."

"Well, you'll be seeing a lot of me. I intend to be a very involved aunt. And with twins, you're going to need all the aunts you can get."

She walked through the joyful throng of people. The big patio doors were thrown open wide so the outdoors was as much a part of the venue as the indoors. Since Marguerite always preferred to be outdoors when she could, she stepped out into the unseasonably warm late October day. She was conscious of a wish to step out of her heels and enjoy the feel of the springy grass under her feet. However, she resisted the urge and remained politely and properly in bridesmaid mode.

For a moment she simply observed. Standing at the edge of the grass field, where there was a slight rise and looked over the groups of people laughing and chatting. A huddle of young girls sat on the grass swapping secrets. Watching them, she experienced a moment of intense nostalgia as she remembered how she and her sisters used to whisper and giggle as kids at a grownup party.

So much had had happened on this piece of land where, through a combination of luck and fate, Daphne and Jack had found themselves, and put down roots and raised eleven children.

Iris stood with Paisley and Dosana, a glass of sparkling water in one hand. The other hand resting protectively on the barely visible mound of her belly. Marguerite glanced once more behind her sister as the group of young girls in their party dresses started giggling.

"Seems like only yesterday we were sitting on that very spot making daisy chains," Rose said, appearing at her side.

"You read my mind."

"So, what's up with you and Alex? He told Matt you were an item, but he's so busy chefing I haven't even seen him yet."

She felt the betrayal all over again. "He told Matt we were an item? I don't think I'm the only one. I caught him kissing Melissa in the food truck."

She was filled with fury all over again so it took a moment to register that Rose was laughing. "You know Melissa's gay, right?"

She turned sharply. "What? Are you sure?"

"Yes. Matt says that's why she and Alex work so well together, because she's not interested in him. Believe me, if she was kissing Alex, it wasn't in lust."

She sighed, turning her engagement ring, which flashed extravagantly when the light hit it. "I probably shouldn't even tell you this, but he asked me if you were seeing anyone. Weeks ago. He's crazy about you."

Geoff emerged from the same patio door she had recently come through herself and she saw the moment he spotted his brand-new bride. As though she felt his gaze upon her, Iris turned toward him. Her smile was the sun on the longest day of the year, and Geoff looked as proud and happy as a man can look.

He strode towards her and, even though she couldn't hear the words, she knew that he was checking in, seeing how she was doing, did she need anything, want anything? She knew he was inclined to fuss a bit but with Iris's background, being always the one who listened to everyone else's troubles and helped them solve their problems that it was nice for her to have a man in her life who wanted to do that for her.

"They sure are happy," Rose said and she nodded in agreement.

She could see that their future would have some rough patches they'd have to wade through as well as all the wonderful moments. Today they were taking a leap of faith, in each other, in the future.

Risk. That's what it came down to. What was love but a risk? Risking your heart, and your happiness, maybe even sometimes your sense of self. She understood that Iris's fears were nothing more than an expression of how deeply she was risking her heart and her happiness. But, if you could ever calculate a risk, Marguerite believed with all her heart that Geoff was a very good risk where Iris was concerned.

While she was watching, Alexei emerged.

He looked so beautiful her breath caught. *Risk* might not be the most terrifying word in her vocabulary. Perhaps *trust* was the word she had trouble with. She didn't want to name the sensation she was feeling but the truth was she did recognize this feeling. It was love.

She had expected love to be sunny days and roses in bloom, laughing and simultaneous orgasms. But she was beginning to realize that love was so much more. It was feeling so deeply connected to another person that she felt his presence when he stepped out of the patio doors. It was wanting him to be happy, even if she wasn't the person who could make him happy. It was believing in him. Believing he could be anything and do anything and, strangely, seeing that when he looked at her he felt the same way.

It was also the pain of knowing that there were no guarantees. On some level she had to trust not only what she was feeling but that Alexei was a man who could be trusted. Trusted with her heart.

"I think you two need to kiss and make up," Rose said before gliding away, the only woman Marguerite knew who could wear Manolo Blahniks across a lumpy grass field and look as though she were strutting down a catwalk.

Alexei seemed to be looking for someone. She watched his gaze skim over Daphne, standing with her hand in Jack's, chatting with some of their neighbors. She saw him pause and watch Iris and Geoff for a second, witnessed her sister raise her right hand, the one that wasn't currently holding a glass of sparkling water and give him the thumbs up sign. He nodded briefly in response and she knew that he was accepting praise on a job well done, one food professional to another. But his steps didn't veer towards any of those groups of people.

And then he turned and saw her standing there watching him. It would've been so easy for her to avert her gaze, walk inside the house, join herself onto one of the other groups scattered around the lawn in happy clumps like recently opened petunias. But she did none of those things. When their gazes connected she didn't drop hers. And she didn't move. For one timeless moment they stood staring at each other. As their gazes connected she felt the sizzle not only of attraction but something deeper and stronger, and then he strode purposely forward to where she was standing.

But Marguerite wasn't the only woman who'd been watching Alexei. One of Geoff's fellow teachers, a very attractive and very single math teacher who looked as though she'd been dipping freely into the punchbowl tottered across the lawn and threw an arm around his waist. While Marguerite watched, the woman leaned up and whispered in his ear. She was tempted to go and rescue him, then realized he'd been handling incidents like this for a long time, when he dexterously removed himself from her arms, said something Marguerite couldn't hear, and gave the woman a hint of a brotherly grin.

The sexy math teacher watched him for a moment, then shrugged, and walked toward James, who was probably the second best looking single man at the wedding.

Alexei pulled up in front of her and for a second just looked at her face. She felt a pulse begin to race and something that felt like dancing butterflies across the skin of her chest. He didn't speak for moment so she began.

"The catering was perfect," she said.

"Thanks." He gazed down at her somewhat ruefully. "Aren't you going to bust my balls for that woman talking to me?"

She opened her eyes wide. "Talking to you? She was so close to you there are drool marks on your shoulder."

"You don't sound mad." But he looked at her somewhat warily as though he wasn't quite sure.

She sighed. "I owe you an apology." It was so hard to say these words, but everything was so clear to her right now that she wanted to share her newfound knowledge with him. "When I saw you kissing Melissa — well, let's just say, it took me back to a time in my life when I was deeply betrayed by someone I loved and trusted. I kind of freaked out."

His eyebrows rose. "Kind of freaked out?"

"Maybe even overreacted," she admitted. "I'm sorry. Obviously, you've worked together a long time and if you wanted to be with her, you'd be with her. I should have listened."

His eyes began to dance. "If I wanted to be with Melissa, I'd need a sex change. She'd been dumped and needed a shoulder. I swear it on my mother's Moussaka. Melissa's in the kitchen if you want to go in and ask her."

She shook her head. "That's okay. I believe you. And I am really happy she's gay. It will make it easier for me knowing you work so closely with her."

He put his head to one side considering her, his hands jammed into his pockets. "So, you're saying that the only women I can talk to are lesbians?" He seemed to consider the possibility. "Or presumably blood relations. You know that could get in the way of my business."

She nodded. "I can see that could be a problem." It was difficult to put her heart out there on a silver platter for him to choose or not choose but she understood that was what she had to do. She'd been wrong and she'd hurt him and she needed to make it right. She hadn't known Melissa was gay, but today, somehow she'd gained enough perspective to see that she'd rushed to make assumptions about Alexei that weren't true. He was a better man than Tim and she'd known it.

So she sucked in a breath and tried to suck up all the courage she could from the land she loved so much and all the rooted plants she'd helped put here, all the strength and stability she could draw from the soil where she had grown up and been happy for so many years. She said, "I have trust issues. And I understand they are my own problem and I need to work on them. So, yes, it's always going to be hard for me when women drape themselves on you and throw themselves at you and offer themselves to you and try to seduce you."

"You know I don't ask for any of that," he said urgently. "It's a curse."

She tried to keep a straight face. "Okay. A curse."

As she gazed into his eyes she could see how much that had to be true and how hard it must be for him. She said, "I know. And I need to trust you more."

"You need to rescue me. If you see me trapped in the grip of some woman, you need to rescue me."

No way she could keep the grin off her face. "Okay."

Then, because he was so adorable and she loved him so much, she said, "I'll make sure you have a wedding ring so big and bright that no woman will be able to ignore it." As she heard the words echo around her she slapped a hand over her mouth. "I mean, that's not what I meant. Words came out of my mouth that I don't even remember forming in my head."

He appeared startled by her words but he didn't turn and run away. Instead, his lips began to curve. "Are you saying what I think you're saying?"

"No! Of course not. That is, if you think I'm

saying what I think you think I'm saying." She was so confused, she added, "I think."

He shook his head. "Well, that's disappointing."

"What's disappointing?"

He took a step back and his gaze dropped to the ground. "I thought, for a second, you were saying you wanted to marry me."

Oh that tricky devil. If she said no, she didn't want to marry him, it was possible he might think she actually didn't want to marry him. When of course there was nothing she wanted more. But she also didn't want to be the one doing the proposing.

For a second there was absolute silence between them. Finally, she said, "I am not putting myself in the position where years from now our grandchildren ask how we ended up married and you get to say that I proposed to you."

He kept his head down but she heard a sound suspiciously like a snort of laughter. "Think about what this is like for me. I'm the one facing rejection here. I mean, you've already rejected me once. I'm not sure I can take it again."

Her eyes narrowed on him. He couldn't see this because he was still looking at the ground but she felt that he was teasing her. But what if he wasn't? No, for once in her life, she was going be strong and ask for what she wanted. She drew herself up to her full height. She sucked in a deep breath. Then he glanced up, and she could see not only the laughter and fun in his eyes but also the piercing light of joy. "Did you say grandchildren?"

She closed her eyes and scrunched up her face as though in pain. "I did. I said grandchildren. This is the effect you have on women. We're not together anymore, we're broken up, and I'm talking to you about grandchildren."

"How many grandchildren are we talking?"

She pulled together the frayed edges of her dignity. "I don't know. I guess that depends on how many children we have."

"Have you been talking to my mother?"

She giggled helplessly. "I adore your mother. She's possibly the only woman I know who makes my mother seem non-interfering."

"It's almost worth getting married just so they have to be in-laws."

She shook her head. "This is not how it goes. We can't talk about in-laws when we aren't even engaged."

"You're right. Someone really needs to finish this proposal. And do it right."

"Well I'm not doing it. I made enough of a fool of myself."

He took her hand and pulled her closer. She raised her head, her heart beating fiercely. She thought he would kiss her but instead he gazed down at her seriously. "I can't promise you that everything will be easy. But I can promise you that I've never loved another woman as I love you and I never will. Before you give me your heart, I ask you to give me your trust."

She dragged in a quick breath. "Can't you ask for something easy? Like all my money or my recipe for pregnant lady tea? Which, by the way, is a closely guarded secret."

He shook his head. Completely serious. "Trust. That's all I want from you."

"You're asking a lot. How am I supposed to just stand there and trust when I see the way women look at you?"

"That's not your business. How do I look at them? As compared to how I look at you? I think you'll find there's a difference."

"But some of those women are so beautiful and sophisticated and smart. Why would you prefer me?"

He put a hand up and gently pushed one of her curls over her shoulder and wrapped his free hand around the cascade falling down her back. "I don't know why. But I do. I will. Forever."

And she understood that this was her moment. It wouldn't always be easy, but if she couldn't trust him they didn't have anything so she nodded slowly. "I promise to trust you with all my ability and if I'm ever unsure about anything to ask you."

"And I will do the same."

She gave a snort of disbelief. "Men don't fall at my feet and salivate when they look at me the way women do to you."

"Yes they do. You just don't see it. Anyway, I promise you the same. I give you my trust and if I'm ever unsure about anything, I will ask."

She nodded. "Deal."

"Good. So we understand each other." He took her arm and began to lead her towards her family. She dug her heels into the ground and halted them. "Wait. Haven't you forgotten something?"

He glanced at her in surprise. "I don't think so."

She dropped her voice. "There's a little matter of a proposal that hasn't been given yet or accepted."

He narrowed his eyes at her. "It was implied."

This was so much fun she could go on for hours but she decided it was time to put a stop to their foolishness. She crossed her hands under her breasts and glared at him. "I want a decent, romantic proposal of marriage and I want it now."

He shook his head. "You drive a hard bargain."

And then, to her shock and surprise, he dropped to one knee at her feet and glanced up at her, lights dancing in his eyes.

She glanced around but so far no one had seen them. "I didn't say you had to get down on one knee."

"Well I'm down here now. If I'm getting grass stains on my pants I want it to mean something."

"Oh stop it. This is the most unromantic thing that's ever happened to me."

She grabbed his hand and tried to yank him up but he held firm. "Marguerite. On the spot where you grew up, and in front of your family and your friends I'm asking you if you would do me the honor of becoming my wife."

His image grew misty as she stared at him through gathering tears. "I didn't think I could love anyone as much as I love you."

"I know the feeling." He stood and took her into his arms and when he kissed her it was possibly the happiest moment of her life. He lifted his head and said, "So, do you think I'll get an answer anytime soon?"

"I'm savoring the moment. But yes. My answer is yes."

"I really didn't see this coming, so I don't have an engagement ring, but I saw this in a jewelry store and I thought of you." He pulled out a silk bag and shook out a ring that sparkled silver in the light. It was a gorgeous hand crafted silver ring set with a fresh water pearl in the center. "Consider it a promise ring." As he slipped it on her ring finger, she felt as though her heart would burst.

Suddenly, a shout rang out. "Okay everybody, gather round, it's time for a toast to the happy couple."

He pulled away and stared down at her startled. "How did the news travel so fast? We haven't even told anyone yet."

She reached up and kissed him softly on the mouth. "The toast isn't for us. It's for Iris and Geoff."

He gazed down at her. "I think the world of your sister and Geoff. But when I drink a toast, it's going be to you and to our future together."

"And I'll be drinking to you and our future. And also to Iris and Geoff. I'll take a very big sip."

"I love you."

"That's a very handy thing, because I love you too."

And, hand in hand, they walked back to join family and friends in celebrating the union of another very happy couple, and the beginning of another generation.

Roots, she mused, as she gazed around at Jack and Daphne and their assorted children. Roots were the basis, and from them grew strong plants that threw out the best and most cherished blooms.

ALSO BY NANCY WARREN

The best way to keep up with new releases, plus enjoy bonus content and prizes is to join Nancy's newsletter at www.nancywarren.net.

TAKE A CHANCE SERIES

Meet the chance family, a cobbled together family of eleven kids who are all grown up and finding their ways in life and love.

Chance Encounter, Prequel
Kiss a Girl in the Rain, Book 1
Iris in Bloom, Book 2
Blueprint for a Kiss, Book 3
Every Rose, Book 4
Love to Go, Book 5

THE ALMOST WIVES CLUB

An enchanted wedding dress is a matchmaker in this series of romantic comedies where five runaway brides find out who the best men really are!

The Almost Wives Club: Kate, Book 1
Second Hand Bride, Book 2

Bridesmaid for Hire, Book 3
The Wedding Flight, Book 4
If the Dress Fits, Book 5

TONI DIAMOND MYSTERIES

Toni is a successful saleswoman for Lady Bianca Cosmetics in this series of humorous cozy mysteries. Along with having an eye for beauty and a head for business, Toni's got a nose for trouble and she's never shy about following her instincts, even when they lead to murder.

Frosted Shadow, Book One
Ultimate Concealer, Book Two
Midnight Shimmer, Book Three

A Diamond Choker For Christmas,
A Toni Diamond Mysteries Novella

For a complete list of books, check out Nancy's website at www.nancywarren.net.

ABOUT THE AUTHOR

Nancy Warren is the USA Today Bestselling author of more than 70 novels. She's originally from Vancouver, Canada, though she tends to wander and has lived in England, Italy and California at various times. Favorite moments include being the answer to a crossword puzzle clue in Canada's National Post newspaper, being featured on the front page of the New York Times when her book Speed Dating launched Harlequin's NASCAR series, and being nominated three times for Romance Writers of America's RITA award. She's an avid hiker, loves chocolate and most of all, loves to hear from readers! The best way to stay in touch is to sign up for Nancy's newsletter at www.nancywarren.net.

Learn more about Nancy and her books:

Twitter: @nancywarren1
Facebook: www.facebook.com/Nancy-Warren
Website: www.nancywarren.net
Email: nancyYwarren@gmail.com